Slocum continued up the fence line until he came to what at first looked like a bundle of rags on the ground. It was a body, and as Slocum carefully turned it over with the toe of his boot, he saw it was a small man who looked Mexican.

"He's dead, and not too long," Slocum said. "He was murdered."

At that moment a shot rang out in the near distance.

"Get down!" Slocum shouted, pushing Lawrence and Harvey to the dirt.

Slocum's trained ears measured the next shot and determined that it was not aimed at them, but rather at the house where Helen Belinda had gone.

In a moment Slocum was on his feet. "Let's go," he said.

"Where are we going?" Harvey Olivier asked.

Slocum looked at him, suddenly grim.

"We're going to help some ladies who need it," Slocum said. "And we're going to start something that I'm afraid will end badly."

DON'T MISS THESE
ALL-ACTION WESTERN SERIES
FROM THE BERKLEY PUBLISHING GROUP

THE GUNSMITH by J. R. Roberts
Clint Adams was a legend among lawmen, outlaws, and
ladies. They called him . . . the Gunsmith.

LONGARM by Tabor Evans
The popular long-running series about U.S. Deputy Marshal
Long—his life, his loves, his fight for justice.

SLOCUM by Jake Logan
Today's longest-running action Western. John Slocum rides
a deadly trail of hot blood and cold steel.

JAKE LOGAN

SLOCUM'S FOLLY

J
JOVE BOOKS, NEW YORK

SLOCUM'S FOLLY

A Jove Book / published by arrangement with
the author

PRINTING HISTORY
Jove edition / September 1996

The Putnam Berkley World Wide Web site address is
http://www.berkley.com

ISBN: 0-515-11940-7

A JOVE BOOK®
Jove Books are published by The Berkley Publishing Group,
200 Madison Avenue, New York, New York 10016.
JOVE and the "J" design are trademarks
belonging to Jove Publications, Inc.

PRINTED IN THE UNITED STATES OF AMERICA

10 9 8 7 6 5 4 3 2 1

1

John Slocum was tired.

Not just his body—he'd been physically tired plenty of times before when his muscles had ached from the days on the run, chased by his past or a more immediately dangerous present. There had been times when, after uncounted hours of riding, his eyes had begun to close, his hands slipped from the reins, his rapier-sharp mind dulled by the sheer drain on his body.

He'd known how to handle that tiredness: a clever hiding place to elude a pursuer, the tricks of his self-imposed trade, catching a few hours of sleep before hitting the saddle again. . . .

But this was different.

He had enough money in his poke to last awhile, if he was careful. So that wasn't it. He even had enough smokes to last awhile, a packet of quirlies in his saddlebag that weren't near to Havanas in pleasure, but good enough. So it wasn't that either. He had enough jerky to last awhile, enough dried biscuits, enough water, enough of everything he needed. . . .

Slocum was just . . . tired.

Tired in spirit.

Maybe I can't cut it anymore, he thought.

Maybe I don't want to.

Other times, when such thoughts had entered his head, Slocum had scoffed and immediately banished them to whatever place the useless things in life were stored. Thoughts like that were good for nothing—they slowed a man down, took the itch from his trigger finger, and eventually would wear him down to the point where he would make that fatal slip; a lag of an instant before pulling the trigger, a twitch of the eye on the rifle sight which gave the opponent the upper hand and ended the game in the enemy's favor. Such thoughts had never stayed long in Slocum's mind, because he had not allowed them to, because they were good for nothing.

But this time . . .

Maybe I'm heading for the end. . . .

Immediately, out of practiced habit, out of self-preservation, Slocum tried to drive the thoughts from his head, but this time they wouldn't leave.

Maybe I should give it up. . . .

I'm tired. . . .

Even the weather here at the edge of the Texas desert had been more of the same: dry sun during the day, cool starry nights with a fattening moon. The same for days.

Under the same moon as every moon, under the

same stars, riding the same saddle and the same Appaloosa, Slocum did something he had never done when riding before.

He yawned. Yawned out of boredom.

Maybe I'll just crawl under a rock, drive out the snakes and scorpions, and sleep for a hundred years. Sleep until . . .

Involuntarily, Slocum yawned again.

Sleep until . . .

Barely keeping his head from drooping onto his chest, Slocum turned his Appaloosa toward a nearing rock outcrop. There in the moonlight was a ledge jutting out over the desert floor, and under it would be a perfect bed.

Sleep until . . .

Shaking himself awake, holding his eyes open against the next yawn, Slocum dismounted, made motions to tie his horse off on a nearby stunted cottonwood, and still yawning, stumbled to the rock ledge, barely ducking his head under. He lay down heavily, his eyes already closing. Somewhere in the back of his mind he chided himself for not unrolling a blanket, for not checking his sleeping spot for rattlers and scorpions, for not checking and feeding his mount, for not checking and cleaning his Colt in its cross-draw holster, for not doing the things he had done every night of his life for the past twenty years.

Sleep until . . .

Vaguely, he knew what he was doing was wrong, and dangerous. He knew that what he was doing was foolhardy and could lead to the thing he had avoided through cleverness, quickness, and cunning all these years: his end.

Don't care, he thought.

Tired . . .

I'll sleep until . . .

2

. . . until something happens . . .

Something was happening.

Slocum's first instinct was to go for his Colt. But he'd rolled over in his sleep, twisting his cross-draw holster beneath him, and while he struggled under the low-hanging rock ledge to right himself he was losing precious seconds.

Serves you right, he thought. *You softened up, and now you're going to die.*

But he didn't die, at least not yet, and the noise that sounded so close to him just went on and didn't get closer. Slocum smelled wood smoke, *green* wood smoke, and heard shouting that sounded like two men arguing. So close that Slocum was sure the men would attack him at any moment. If only he could turn around and see . . .

Finally Slocum jerked his body around and looked out into the nearby moonlit landscape.

At first he saw nothing but a cloud of smoke, and heard the shouts of the two men. Still trying to get his Colt out of its holster, Slocum desperately tried to peer through the smoke, to catch sight of the two men, to see what they were up to—

Suddenly a body rolled out of the green wood smoke toward Slocum and came to rest against him, pinning Slocum tightly into the back of his sleeping spot.

Suddenly eye-to-eye with one of his attackers, Slocum looked into a skinny face topped by a dusty Easterner's derby hat. The stranger's face went suddenly blank before the man suddenly smiled stupidly, his eyes crinkling, and said, "Hello!"

"Get away from me!" Slocum shouted, pushing the stranger back away, knocking the derby hat off. Slocum managed to reach his Colt and yanked it out, holding it on the befuddled skinny fellow as he climbed out of the rock ledge and stood up, still holding the weapon on his opponent, who merely sat on the ground, staring up at him and now moving his fingers through his ridiculous upstanding crown of hair.

Again the stranger smiled up at him, saying nothing, and suddenly the man shrugged, crinkling his eyes again as his smile broadened, until he abruptly focused his attention on Slocum's six-shooter. The stranger frowned, opened his mouth as if to say something, then suddenly keeled over in a dead faint.

"I told you—!" a voice yelled from within the thick wood smoke, and now the second stranger, a huge round fellow dressed in clothing similar to the first, emerged from the smoke to confront Slocum.

The second stranger, his face blossoming in alarm, looked from Slocum to his unconscious companion on the ground, then back to Slocum again.

"You didn't . . ." the stranger said, pointing from Slocum's gun to the unconscious man.

"No," Slocum said, "I didn't shoot him. But maybe I should have."

The rotund stranger ignored Slocum's gun, moved forward, and held out his hand, a beaming smile on his face.

"Perhaps I should introduce myself," the fat stranger said. "I am Mr. Harvey Olivier, and this," he said, with exaggerated formality indicating his friend, who now stirred from his unconscious state and sat up, pushing up his ridiculous hair with his fingers again, "is Mr. Lawrence Stanwell. We are gentlemen of distinction, here to make our fortune, and pleased to make your acquaintance."

Realizing just how harmless these two fools were, Slocum put his Colt back into its holster and held out his hand.

"And you are?" the fat man asked, with profound politeness. Slocum noticed the Southern accent in the man's voice.

"Slocum. John Slocum."

"Now that's a funny name, don't you think?" the skinny one, still sitting in the dust, said to the fat one. His accent was faintly British. "Slocum John Slocum?"

The fat one looked confused for a moment, then,

as realization dawned, looked down on his compatriot with scorn.

"That's not his name, you dolt! It's John Slocum!"

"Then why does he call himself Slocum John Slocum?" the skinny one asked.

The fat one threw up his hands in despair and turned to Slocum.

"Please make allowances for my friend, Mr. Slocum," he said. "Sometimes he gets..." He rolled his eyes.

"That's quite all right," Slocum said. "But do you think you could let go of my hand now?"

With acute embarrassment, Mr. Olivier looked down to see that he was still shaking Slocum's hand.

"Pardon me," he said with a little laugh, taking his hand away.

"Is he a judge?" Stanwell said blankly. "You asked him to pardon you."

Roaring with impatience, Olivier stepped over to Stanwell, hauled him to his feet, and said, "Will you please not be so stupid!"

Stanwell regarded him sternly for a moment, then seemed to lose track of what he was thinking and reverted to a blank stare.

"Mr. Slocum," Olivier pleaded, "we're sorry for any inconvenience we caused you." He made a short bow. "We'll be on our way..."

With that he took Stanwell roughly by the arm and proceeded to walk back into the thick smoke which still issued from their nearby fire.

3

"Just a minute," Slocum said, intrigued, and trying not to laugh.

The two dandies turned around.

"Yes?" Olivier said.

"Just what is it you two are up to?"

"Why," Olivier said, "we're heading toward our fortune, of course."

"Yeah," Stanwell said, pointing to his friend. "We're going to be rich beyond your wildest dreams." He thought for a moment and corrected himself. "*Our* wildest dreams."

"Rich, eh?" Slocum said.

"That's right," Olivier said. "We've come West to claim our fortune in the ranch our good friend left us."

"Yeah," Stanwell said, nodding with conviction again. "He's dead."

"Your friend is dead?"

"That's right," Stanwell said. "Shot with a bullet and everything."

Olivier spoke up. "We shouldn't burden this man with our troubles."

"Why not?" Stanwell said. "We've got plenty to spare."

"That's all right," Slocum said. "I'd like to hear what you're up to. Also, I'd like to know what two dudes like you are doing out here alone in the middle of Mescalero country. Do you realize you could get scalped?"

Stanwell's face filled with terror. "But Harvey," he said, suddenly bawling like a baby, "I don't want to get sculpted! It could hurt when they hit you with that chisel, and—"

In exasperation, Olivier said, "Not sculpted, *scalped*!"

Halting his crying in an instant, Stanwell smiled and said, "Oh, that's not so bad."

As Slocum looked on in amusement, Olivier explained to his friend what scalping was, which resulted in all the color leaving Stanwell's face, before he fainted again.

"Excuse me," Olivier said, bending down to tend to his friend. Shaking his head and smiling, Slocum went to his mount and drew out his bourbon flask, returned to Olivier, and handed it to him.

"Give him some of this," he said.

Nodding his thanks, Olivier held the open flask to Stanwell's lips.

The skinny man's eyes flew open in shock, and in an instant he was on his feet, eyes still wide open.

"Bring on the scalpers!" he said, trying to take

the flask from Olivier's hands. The fat man pulled it away and gave it back to Slocum, with thanks.

"And now we'll be on our way," Olivier said.

Stanwell punched at the empty air. "Bring on the scalpers! And the sculptors, too!"

"You two have water? And food?" Slocum asked.

Olivier knitted his brow. "Why, no."

"Weapons? A rifle, a six-shooter?"

Still frowning, as Stanwell stumbled off into the wood smoke, Olivier shook his head.

"Horses? A wagon?"

"Nothing like that," Olivier said.

"Then how the hell did you get out here?" Slocum asked in astonishment.

"We rode here," Olivier said. "A nice gentleman in a wagon took us this far, and said a stagecoach would be by for us in the morning."

"Was he laughing when he said it?"

"Why, yes, he was," Olivier said.

Shaking his head, Slocum sighed tiredly. "You two have been had," he said. "There hasn't been a stage out this way since time began."

"But he was even kind enough to sell us the wood for our fire!" Olivier protested.

Now feeling unaccountably alive again because of the antics of this fat fellow and his friend, Slocum said, "Where is it you need to get to?"

"Why, Parsonage, Texas."

"It's only a half day's ride from here," Slocum said. He still did not quite understand why all the feelings of tiredness and boredom he had felt a few short hours before were suddenly gone, vanished into the green wood smoke with the appearance of these two clowns. But perhaps he understood a little when the skinny one, Lawrence Stanwell, now lurched comically out of the smoke, coughing and falling down at the foot of his friend. In any case, Slocum added, "Come on, I'll get you there."

4

"We really can't thank you enough, Mr. Slocum," Harvey Olivier said a few hours later, after Slocum had made them wait for sunup before continuing their journey. In the interim, Slocum had built a real fire, shared his jerky and water, and watched with amusement while Lawrence Stanwell puffed and then choked on one of Slocum's quirlies, which he'd rolled for the man.

Now they had broken camp, and in deference to the two strangers, Slocum walked with them, leading his Appaloosa.

He was amazed at their stupidity. Between the two of them, Slocum reckoned they had three dollars and little else, except for a few possessions: a harmonica, which Lawrence played excruciatingly badly, to the point where Harvey had knocked it from the skinny man's hands to the ground; a pair of wax apples, one of which evidenced a bite, about which Harvey would say nothing except, "Never mind," while rolling his eyes; a magazine in

German, which neither of the men understood, but about which Lawrence said, with his idiotic smile, "I liked the pictures," of which there were none. These and a few other meager items were rolled in a bandanna and carried at the end of a stick by Lawrence Stanwell. The men were horrifically dressed for the country, in ties, vests, suits, and Eastern shoes with holes in them. Slocum was amazed they had made it this far alive.

And yet there was something endearing about them, something that made Slocum smile. The fat one was pompous and fussy but not overbearing, and the skinny one was so helpless that he invited help.

"I can't tell you how much we appreciate your company, Mr. Slocum," Olivier said as they trudged through the morning, which was growing increasingly hot. Still, the two men refused to remove their derbies, which somehow looked natural on their heads.

"Don't mention it," Slocum said, somehow happy for the company himself.

"All right," said Lawrence, "we won't." He pointed to his fat friend. "But he already has."

Olivier merely threw his hands up in exasperation.

By noon it was plenty hot, and still the town of Parsonage refused to appear in front of them. Even Slocum, in much better shape than these two dudes, was tired of walking.

"Why don't you tell me your story?" Slocum said.

Lawrence looked at him with puzzlement, and then shrugged and said, "All right. You see, once there was a little girl named Red Riding Hood—"

"Not *a* story!" his fat friend shouted. "He wants to hear *our* story!"

Puzzlement came back to Lawrence's face. "But that *is* my story. My aunt used to tell it to me when I was little, as I sat on her knee."

Olivier pushed Lawrence, who went sprawling in the dust. When he stood up, straightening his hat and dusting himself off, he continued to walk, still puzzled.

Olivier pointed to himself. "*I* will tell Mr. Slocum our story."

"Suit yourself," Lawrence said. "But I still like Little Red Riding Hood."

Shaking his head, Olivier turned to Slocum. "As I said, we are travelers from the East." He laughed fussily. "Temporarily unemployed."

"Yeah," Lawrence chimed in, "and we are out of work too."

Fixing his friend with a momentary stare, Olivier went on. "As I said, temporarily unemployed. And then the most amazing bit of luck overtook us. As we walked past what you would call out in these parts a 'saloon,' a gentleman came out and stumbled into us. I would hesitate to say he was inebriated, but he *did* claim to be our long-lost best friend, and within minutes had convinced us of this amazing fact by selling us his most treasured possession—a ranch out here in Texas!''

"Is that so," Slocum said, already suspicious. "And how much did he sell it to you for?''

"Why, for only ten dollars!''

"And how much did you have at the time?''

"Eleven dollars!'' Lawrence chimed in. "He let us keep the other dollar for traveling expenses. We bought our firewood with it!''

"That's right," said Olivier. "He gave us a deed, and then went back into the saloon, and before you knew it, he came out again.''

"Yeah," said Lawrence, "only this time he had a bullet hole in him.''

"Isn't that amazing?'' Olivier said. "And he stumbled toward us, with his hand out, only he fell down and died as I shook it.''

"And his famous last words were 'snake.' ''

"Snake?'' Slocum asked.

"That's right," Olivier said, befuddled. "He said 'snake,' and then he passed on.''

"And then we heard the snake, and ran!'' Lawrence said.

"That's right, we heard the snake, a hissing sound, and we ran! And that very night we hid in a train car, and came out West to claim our good fortune!''

"And here we are!'' Lawrence said.

"That's right!'' Olivier said, very pleased with himself.

"That's some story," Slocum said.

"You bet it is," Lawrence said. "Almost as good as Little Red Riding Hood!"

"You have the deed?" Slocum asked.

"Show it to him," Olivier said eagerly.

Lawrence looked blankly at his friend.

"But you have it," he said.

"No, *you* have it," Olivier countered.

Lawrence said, "No, you have it."

"No, *you* have it!"

Angry now, Lawrence swung the stick holding the bandanna holding all the duo's worldly possessions at his friend, and the bandanna loosened, its contents flying out.

"*Now* look at what you've done!" Olivier said.

Slocum bent to pick up a folded piece of paper which had fallen out.

"Is this the deed?" he said, holding it up.

"What, yes!" Olivier said. "But how did you get it!"

"He's a magician!" Lawrence said.

Slocum unfolded the paper, and while the two men gathered their belongings back into the bandanna, studied the deed, which had been signed over to the boys by a man named Carver. To his surprise, it looked genuine.

"Looks like you dudes own a ranch," he said.

"You see?" Olivier said, taking the paper back and putting it in his pocket.

Slocum stopped walking. "This looks like a good enough place to eat."

He began to rifle through his saddlebags for jerky and hard biscuits, while Lawrence emptied

out the bandanna again and tied it around his neck
as a napkin.

"And now I can tell you *my* story!" Lawrence
said happily, while his fat friend only rolled his
eyes.

5

After lunch and more foolishness, they began to walk again. Slocum was becoming concerned that they hadn't reached Parsonage yet, but kept it to himself.

Around three o'clock a wagon appeared from the east, behind them, and as it steadily drew closer Slocum thought it prudent to walk next to his mount, near his Winchester's saddle scabbard. While his two companions prattled on, Slocum kept an eye on the wagon.

But as it drew close Slocum saw there was little cause for alarm. The wagon held seven ladies, dressed for business—and the one at the reins looked to Slocum as if she could handle herself. She was full-figured, with hair as black as night and eyes that looked like they could be mean as daggers or soft as moonlight. She kept her eyes on Slocum as the wagon pulled alongside.

"You gonna shoot us?" she said, smiling slightly.

"Not likely, ma'am," Slocum said.

"Good, then I won't shoot you either," she said, putting down the sawed-off rifle she had hidden in her petticoats.

She nodded toward Lawrence and Harvey, who were looking at the tittering ladies in the wagon while smiling shyly and shuffling their feet.

"What's with the dudes?"

Slocum smiled. "You got that part right. They own a ranch over in Parsonage, and have come out to make their claim on it."

"You don't say!" the lady said. Slocum knew she was measuring him, and knew she approved of what she saw. "That wouldn't be the Carver place, would it?"

"Why, yes!" Harvey Olivier said, and then reverted to shyness. "That is, yes, ma'am, it would be."

Lawrence curtsied, while the painted ladies continued to titter.

"Well, I'll be," the lady with the reins said. "We'd heard tell that Carver might have given the place away before his demise. I'd tell you gentlemen, all three of you, to be careful about that property." She held her hand out to Slocum.

"My name's Helen Belinda," she said.

Slocum took her hand, which was surprisingly delicate and soft.

"John Slocum," he said.

"I thought your name was Slocum John Slocum!" Lawrence said suddenly.

Olivier pushed his friend, who fell down, sending the painted ladies in the wagon into a further tittering fit.

Helen Belinda kept her eyes on Slocum.

"I hope we'll be seeing more of you," she said, her slight smile returning.

"Could be, ma'am," Slocum said, smiling slightly himself. "I've more or less promised to get these two fellows settled into their new ranch."

"Is that so?" Helen Belinda said. She nodded. "Good for them that you're around. Like I said, there's apt to be trouble over that property, but you look like you can handle yourself."

"I can handle myself," Slocum said.

"I bet you can," Helen Belinda said. "But in the meantime," she continued, turning to Harvey and Lawrence, "why don't you two dudes get in the back of the wagon, and Mr. Slocum can ride that fine horse of his, and I'll take you into Parsonage."

"That would be fine, ma'am," Slocum said while Harvey and Lawrence, bumping into one another, scrambled to climb up into the wagon with the still-tittering ladies. "Thank you."

Helen Belinda turned her smile on Slocum again.

"Oh, you might have plenty to thank me for later," she said.

6

It turned out that Parsonage, Texas, had a familiar look to Slocum when the small town spread itself out in front of them as they topped the next rise. Parsonage was small, dusty, and desperate, a way stop south of the Southern Pacific Railroad that had probably once thrived when stagecoaches were the only lifeline in the West. Now it looked about to give up, as many of the smaller towns well off the rail lines already had.

"Used to be a nice little place," Helen Belinda said in confirmation of what Slocum thought. "I grew up not too far from here, before Parsonage became a cattle town. Used to be a few farmers, mostly folks wanting to get away from Abilene or Fort Worth. Now cattle's the only game in town, and Bart Forsen is the only man with cattle."

She turned to look at Lawrence and Harvey, who sat red-faced and shy in the back of the wagon while the girls tittered over them.

"Except for you two dudes," Helen said.

"Pardon me, ma'am?" Harvey Olivier said.

"I said, you two dandies are the only ones around here 'cept Forsen who own cattle."

"Is that right?" Slocum said, interested.

Helen laughed. "But don't get too excited about it. There aren't that many left, and, well . . . let's just say the Bar B Ranch ain't what it used to be."

She laughed again, and so did the girls.

Harvey looked puzzled.

"But Mr. Carver told us the ranch was a little piece of heaven!"

Again, Helen laughed. "Well, Carver was nothing if not a good storyteller."

"But what—" Harvey began.

"You'll find out soon enough," Helen said.

Soon they were driving through Parsonage, and drawing their share of attention. The ladies certainly drew their share, but Lawrence and Harvey, with their Eastern clothes, drew just as much eyeballing from the locals, who stopped their sweeping or shopkeeping to stand out in the dust and gawk.

"Gentleman, I think you've made a hit!" Helen said.

Slocum noticed that her demeanor changed when they passed the sheriff's office and the lawman came out to stare at them. He looked like an unpleasant enough character, the kind of seedy, mustached, slant-eyed figure Slocum had crossed paths with all too many times. Slocum knew the type immediately—either a former desperado or Army man, he had reached the bottom with a badge in a one-horse town. Quite probably he was a drunk and a lout, but he would be smart, because he knew that this was his last chance to corner himself a piece of the world. He'd know how to hang onto that piece, and would be mean if crossed. Also he would probably be in the pocket of the local rich man, probably this cattle baron Forsen that Helen had mentioned.

"Sheriff Rowles," Helen Belinda said in an unfriendly voice as they passed.

The sheriff kept his hard eyes on them, then walked back into his office and closed the door.

"Trouble there?" Slocum said.

"And it won't take long," Helen said.

Slocum waited for her to go on, but for the first time he noticed a break in her ready-for-the-world demeanor.

"Anything I can do?" Slocum said.

She looked at him, and her smiled came back.

"Like I said—later," she told him.

7

As quickly as they began their ride through Parsonage, it was over, and they headed out on the rough road before Helen Belinda turned off on an even rougher one, a mere set of worn ruts in the dusty road.

"Are we almost there?" Harvey Olivier asked from the back.

"Not hardly," Helen said. "And I wouldn't be in too much of a hurry if I were you!"

Lawrence smiled and said, "Yeah, we're going to be rich, and we don't want to be in a hurry about it!"

Helen smiled and shook her head.

And they kept going. Soon Parsonage was a mere memory behind them, and Slocum was getting tired of being in the saddle, when a beautiful sight spread itself before them. Inside a beautifully tended fence spread one of the finest grazing areas Slocum had ever seen. It spread for miles, fine grass on gently sloping hills, and as they topped another rise Slocum saw a magnificent herd of cattle, fine beefsteak on the hoof, healthy as lambs and grazing to their heart's content. In the dim distance was a fine ranch house, two-storied and looking to be nearly an acre in size by itself.

"The Bar B Ranch!" Lawrence shouted, and his fat companion sat stunned beside him, his mouth open.

"It's . . . beautiful," Harvey said, tears coming to his eyes.

"It sure is," Helen Belinda said, "but it ain't yours. That's Bart Forsen's place, the Forsen Ranch,'bout the finest in this part of the state."

"I believe it," Slocum said.

A hard look came into Helen's eyes.

"Didn't used to be quite as big," she said. "In fact," she continued, pointing to a spot to the left of the magnificent ranch house, where a bunkhouse, one-storied but nearly as large as the main structure, stood, "that's where my daddy's spread used to be. And over there," she continued, pointing farther off to the left, "was Sid Marchant's ranch, and behind his was the Peters place."

"I take it Bart Forsen's been buying up property?" Slocum said, already knowing the answer.

Helen's eyes were still hard. "You might say that. If bullets are considered hard cash."

"He shot his neighbors?"

"Nothing to prove," Helen said. " 'Specially not when the sheriff is one of your cronies, and the local judge is your brother, who looks at shots in the back as self-defense, and when half Forsen's

neighbors decided to move out rather than die."
She smiled grimly. "He made them good offers, of
course. At least in the beginning. After a while he
figured he didn't even have to do that. After Bob
Peters' brother went and got himself killed from
Forsen's 'self-defense,' I think Forsen offered Bob
five gold pieces for his place. It was the second
biggest around here, nearly as large a spread as
Forsen already had."

"And what about you?" Slocum said.

For the first time Slocum saw anger flash in her
eyes.

"What do you mean?" she asked.

"What did Forsen take from you?"

"Nothing I want to talk about," she said
quickly.

Slocum said, "I only meant—"

Her tone softened. "I've got my own business
with Forsen, but it's none of your concern, John
Slocum."

"Maybe I could help."

"I don't think I'd want that. Like I said, it's my
own affair. It's nothing I want to talk about now
anyway," she said, and then turned her eyes back
to the wagon's horse and drove them on until they
were past the Forsen Ranch and still going.

After a while she turned to Slocum, and smiled
again.

"But I do appreciate the offer," she said.

8

And then finally, after what seemed another day of riding, when even the Forsen spread was well behind them and nearly invisible, they topped a final rise and Helen Belinda called out, "There it is, boys!"

At first Lawrence and Harvey could see nothing; even Slocum could make out only a vague hint of something in the near distance that seemed to blend in too well with the dusty surroundings.

Helen Belinda said, "That there is the Bar B Ranch, boys!"

And then Slocum made it out—a tottering ranch house, leaning to one side, with gaping holes in its roof, surrounded by acres of dust and broken fence.

"That?" Slocum said.

Lawrence and Harvey were staring, mouths open.

Helen snapped the reins, and the wagon soon pulled into the ranch, under a sign missing all but the letters "CH" at the end of "RANCH," supported on two rickety posts leaning to either side, which twisted away from one another, dropping the sign and the two letters to the ground, as the wagon passed through.

Harvey looked at the sign.

"Well, *that* will have to be fixed!" he said.

"That ain't all," Slocum said, nodding at the ranch house, which loomed before them.

Helen Belinda stopped the wagon in front of the house and sat laughing. The girls in the back chuckled as Lawrence and Harvey got down and began to rummage among the wreckage. A table supported on one end by crates stood in the front yard; next to it was a chair, which collapsed when Lawrence sat down on it. He sat stunned, blinking in confusion, and his fat friend stood over him in disgust.

"Will you *stop* this foolishness!" Harvey said. "Let's go inside and see what there is to see."

"Don't know if I'd do that," Slocum said.

"Why, what do you mean?" Harvey said. "We own it, don't we?"

"Sure, you own it," Slocum said, "but I don't think it'll last very long. That roof looks like it's about to go over at any minute."

"Preposterous!" Harvey blustered. "It just needs a little cosmetic work is all. Lawrence, come with me!"

With that the fat man hauled his skinny friend to his feet, and the two of them marched up the front steps, which splintered and broke away at each step, forcing the men to pull themselves up onto the front porch, which creaked ominously.

"Just a little setback!" Harvey said, twirling his tie. "Come, Lawrence!"

And then the two men, side by side, marched into the house, which, amazingly, stood intact.

"You see!" Harvey called out. "It's perfectly safe!"

With that, there was a tremendous roar, and the roof caved in, along with the walls. There was a cry of dismay from within, and a moment later Lawrence and Harvey, covered from head to foot in dust and debris, stood in the midst of the complete wreckage of what had been their ranch house.

Staring blankly for a moment, Lawrence suddenly bent down and picked up a brass lantern, miraculously untouched, its glass intact.

He smiled, holding up his treasure.

"Look!" he said.

The bottom of the lamp fell out, dropping the glass to the ground, where it shattered into a thousand shards.

Harvey looked at Lawrence for a moment.

"Must you destroy *everything* you touch?" Harvey asked.

His friend began to whimper, then cry. "Well, I didn't mean it, it just broke!"

Trying to keep his dignity, the fat man began to stroll through the wreckage toward Slocum, Helen Belinda, and the girls, who were trying very hard not to laugh.

Harvey stopped midway to look back at Lawrence, who still stood whimpering.

"Well, are you coming or not?" Harvey demanded.

Lawrence nodded and took a step forward, his foot finding a loose board which jerked up and hit him, knocking him backward in a heap.

He sat up, covered in even more dust, and began to fluff up his hair with his fingers.

When his fat friend glowered at him, he just shrugged.

"*This* is the way to walk!" Harvey said huffily, putting his foot down and finding a board of his own, which popped up and smacked him flat on the nose.

"Owww!" Harvey bellowed, rubbing at his nose.

"You see!" Lawrence called out. "It's not so easy after all!"

Harvey glowered murderously at his friend, while Slocum and the others, looking on, watched in amazement. It didn't seem possible to Slocum that anyone could be so clumsy or accident-prone.

Time would prove him wrong, however.

9

"The way I see it," Slocum said later, when the two dudes had finally made their way out of the debris and dusted themselves off, "you'll have to build from scratch."

"But we haven't got any money!" Harvey said.

Slocum pondered. "Well, you can tent it for a while, and we can probably salvage enough from that wreck to build some type of shack to get you going. The fences'll have to be mended." He turned to Helen Belinda. "You think there're any cattle in this deal?"

"That's where you're in luck," Helen said. "Nate Carver knew nothing about ranch houses, but he sure as hell knew about cattle. The fences down around here are a mess, but you'll find up over the next hill some of the best grazing land around here, and that includes Bart Forsen's land. And the last time I was out here the fences over there were in good shape, and there were a couple of hundred head of cattle grazing on that land."

"Is that so?"

Helen nodded. "Before Carver hightailed it out East, he hired himself a Mexican fellow name of Franco to tend to the herd. If he ain't been run off by Forsen, I'm sure he's still doing his job." She looked at the wreck of the ranch house. "He was smart enough not to stay here. You'll prob'ly find him out there tomorrow."

She looked at the sky, which had begun to darken.

"Well, me and the girls still got a little ridin' to do, so we'll say our good-byes for now!"

Slocum said, "Where are you heading?"

She nodded up past where they had traveled. "My daddy's old place, at least for tonight. Forsen owns it now, but I don't think he'll chase us off. If he tries, I've got my sawed-off rifle to help persuade him he should be kind. Tomorrow we go back into Parsonage to set up shop."

"You're shopkeepers?" Lawrence said brightly, grinning.

"In a manner of speaking, honey," Helen said. The girls tittered.

Lawrence looked perplexed, while his fat friend, Harvey, turned red and looked embarrassed.

"Well, you certainly are lovely ladies!" Harvey said.

"Thanks," Helen said. She turned to Slocum and put out her hand.

"I'll be seeing more of you, I hope," she said.

Slocum noticed that as he shook her hand, which

was soft and slim, she looked directly into his eyes and gave him her slight ironic smile.

"Maybe I'll be seeing you sooner than you think," she said.

"Whatever you say, ma'am," Slocum said.

"All right, girls! Let's go!" Helen Belinda said, and in a moment she had climbed up into the wagon, the other ladies gathering in the back.

Helen Belinda snapped the reins, and in a cloud of dust the wagon was gone.

Lawrence looked after them, confused.

"I still don't understand what kind of shop they're going to keep," he said.

Throwing up his hands in exasperation, Harvey said, "Never mind."

"But if they don't keep a shop, how can they keep shop?" Lawrence asked. "Don't you have to keep something in your shop if you're a shop-keeper?"

His fat friend looked at him and shook his head.

"In a hundred years, you'd never grow any smarter," Harvey said, sighing.

"Oh, I don't know," Lawrence answered. "In a hundred years we might all be smarter."

"Why is that?"

"Well," Lawrence said, "you see, in a hundred years, our brains would be a hundred years older, and . . ."

He seemed to lose himself in his thoughts.

"I'm waiting," Harvey said.

"Well, if you had a hundred years and you had a brain . . ."

Suddenly the skinny man threw up his hands in befuddlement, his eyes going blank.

"Just as I thought," Harvey said. "Why, do you know that, without me, you wouldn't know how to walk straight?"

Lawrence's befuddlement changed to resolve. "Oh, yeah?"

Lawrence walked straight, and suddenly tripped over his own feet and fell down.

"That's not fair!" Lawrence shouted, angry.

"What's not fair?"

"The ground reached up and grabbed me!"

Harvey rolled his eyes. "I rest my case," he said.

"You two dudes want something to eat?" Slocum said.

"Yes, sir!" Lawrence said, and as he got up he bumped into Harvey, and soon the two men were rolling on the ground, trying to get out of each other's way, while Slocum looked on, shaking his head.

10

As the sun was lipping the western horizon and stars began to dot the east, Slocum helped the two dudes erect a crude lean-to using parts from the wreck of their house.

"That'll do for now," Slocum said, putting the last slat of the primitive but effective structure in place. "Maybe tomorrow we can get you started on something more permanent. You'll be okay here."

"And what about you, Mr. Slocum?" Harvey Olivier asked while his skinny companion looked on blankly. "Where will you sleep?"

"Oh, don't worry about me. I'll sleep out under the stars. Done that often enough. Besides," he said, grinning to himself, "the coyotes and rattlers'll go after you two, and I'll be left alone."

Harvey and Stanwell's eyes went wide.

"Just kidding, boys," Slocum said. "Nothing out here'll bother you. And I won't be far away, so don't worry."

"Mr. Slocum?" Stanwell said, his face screwed up as if he were about to cry.

"What is it?"

"If you hear a snake, will you come running?"

"Yeah," Olivier said, "like I told you, we heard that snake hiss back in New York, just before Mr. Carver was killed."

Waving his hand as he walked away, Slocum said, "Sure, boys, I'll come running. Don't you worry."

Stanwell was whining, "Snakes, oh, snakes . . ."

"Oh, will you stop it!" Olivier shouted, and Slocum heard them begin their fighting as he walked on, before there was a loud "Owwwwww!" from Olivier, followed by a crash.

Slocum returned to find the lean-to in a shambles, Lawrence and Olivier lying in a heap in the midst of it.

"Sorry, Mr. Slocum," Olivier said meekly.

"Yeah, sorry," Lawrence added.

"Get up out of there," Slocum said sternly, and after he had finished with the structure he lectured the two fools. "And this time if you knock it down, you can sleep out in the open and the snakes can get you for all I care!"

He stalked off, only half annoyed, and noted with satisfaction that the two idiots had already started to fight again before he was out of earshot.

Slocum chose a spot far enough from the other two so that he could just hear them in case something went really wrong.

He didn't expect anything to happen this night. He didn't think Bart Forsen, the cattle baron, would start anything this soon. He had no doubt there'd be trouble, and soon, but not this night.

But that didn't keep Slocum from his routine. Before bedding down he had his Winchester at the ready nearby, and his Colt also, and only then did he settle down to dream under the stars. . . .

And awoke with a start in the night. Even in his dreams he reacted, had trained himself to react to the sound of movement. He would have been dead years ago if he hadn't.

Instantly his hand was on his Colt, pointed at the figure looming over him in the darkness.

"Shhhh," the figure said, leaning down to brush a soft hand across his face.

"I told you I'd see you soon enough, John Slocum."

"Helen Belinda?" Slocum said, almost ready to release pressure on the trigger of the gun.

"The one and only," Helen Belinda cooed, and it was certainly she. Only she was dressed only in a robe, her raven-black hair framing her smiling face in the darkness.

"How . . ." Slocum began, but then he saw the wagon stopped a good thirty yards off, near the entrance to the Bar B Ranch.

Helen laughed gently, and drew the robe back from her shoulders till it fell to the ground, revealing her creamy nakedness beneath.

Now Slocum released the pressure on his Colt's

trigger, and laid the weapon down as pressure began to build on his other trigger.

"Nice to see you again, ma'am," he said. "All of you, that is."

Helen Belinda leaned down over to kiss him, all the while loosening Slocum's belt to explore beneath.

"Why, Mr. Slocum, I do believe you're glad to see me."

"You could say that, ma'am."

"Call me Helen."

"Helen, then," Slocum said, gasping as her expert fingers pulled him free and began to stroke.

"Hell," Helen growled in sexual heat. "Call me ready," she said, lowering herself impatiently over Slocum's hard and ready shaft and dropping wet and hot around it.

Both Slocum and Helen Belinda moaned softly, as Slocum felt himself driven deep and deeper within her.

She began to move atop him, pulling him deeper and harder still, as Slocum began to explore her hard-nippled breasts with his hands, and then moved down her flat hard belly and around to her creamy rump, holding a beautiful cheek with each hand while she bucked above him like a rodeo rider.

"Quite . . . a . . . ride, Mr. Slocum!" Helen Belinda gasped.

"Whatever you . . . like . . ." Slocum said.

"I . . . like it . . . *now*!" Helen Belinda said.

Slocum felt the tide rise from his balls and into

the base of his love shaft, and let it build until he could hold it no more.

"Here it comes!" he said.

And it did, a raging torrent of white cum that shot up into her as she drove deep down around him. She was nearly thrown off the sex horse that was Slocum, so forceful was his load driven into her. She cried in deep pleasure, her hands gripping Slocum's own on her butt as one volley and then another and another still drove into her.

And now as Slocum still shot, Helen Belinda's own orgasm kicked in, picking up where Slocum's left off to ravage Slocum's cock in sweet hot wet rivers of her own making.

And now, finally, they each fired their own last volley together, Slocum pushing his rear end up off the ground to grind her even deeper as she held and strained against him, pulling every last drop of white cum from Slocum and mingling it with her own sweet juice.

Now she fell away from him, exhausted, leaving Slocum's covered slick member as happy as Slocum himself.

"My, my," Slocum said, smiling.

"That was . . . wonderful . . ." Helen Belinda said, nearly breathless. "You're as good as I thought you would be, John."

She looked over at him, her face beautiful in star and moonlight.

"Even better," she cooed.

And then Slocum felt her snaking fingers find his still-half-hard member, and begin to harden it fully again, using the slickness that still covered it.

"And I imagine," she said, rising over him again as her strength returned and his also, "that you'll be be just as good the second time."

"And the third," Slocum said, and Helen Belinda laughed sweetly, before going to work again.

"And fourth?" she gasped a moment later, and Slocum smiled, knowing she meant it.

11

Helen Belinda had meant it all right, and when Slocum awoke, still smiling, the next morning, she was gone. Slocum vaguely remembered her whispering, "Thank you, John," before leaving him exhausted and content sometime before dawn. A little later he had heard her wagon pulling away.

And now it was well past sunup, and Slocum smelled coffee and bacon and eggs, and thought he was still in a dream.

He rose up on his elbows, moving painfully with the memory of the previous evening's entertainment, and rubbing his eyes to make sure he was awake, beheld, near the lean-to he had built for the two dudes, the amazing sight of a campfire of non-green wood, a coffeepot and a sizzling frying pan hanging over it.

"Well, I'll be," Slocum said.

"Oh, Mr. Slocum!" Harvey Olivier called out cheerfully. "Your breakfast is ready!"

Slocum called back, "And I'm ready for it!"

He rose gingerly, wincing at the soreness in his overworked muscles, and ambled over to where Lawrence and Harvey had set a table and produced three chairs.

"How—" Slocum began, but a jolly Harvey Olivier cut him off before he could speak.

"Tut, tut, Mr. Slocum!" Harvey scolded fussily. "It was our pleasure to make you breakfast! After all you've done for us! Please," he said, affecting the ways of a waiter and pulling out a chair at the table for Slocum, "sit down and enjoy!"

Still wondering if perhaps he was in a dream, Slocum sat down and allowed Harvey to hand him a linen napkin.

"Coffee?" Harvey said brightly.

"Sure."

"Coming right up! Oh, Lawrence!"

Lawrence Stanwell appeared, covered in broken eggs and feathers, looking confused.

"What happened to you?" Harvey said.

Lawrence held his hands out in bewilderment. "Well, there were no more eggs in the henhouse, so I tried to get some more directly from the chickens!"

"Directly from the chickens indeed!" Harvey said. "Why, don't you know you have to wait for the chickens to *lay* the eggs?"

"*Now* you tell me," Lawrence said, while Harvey sighed in consternation.

Slocum laughed, and Harvey Olivier returned to being the fussy waiter, pouring coffee from the pot into an almost unchipped mug, and then producing a plate of bacon and eggs, which he took from the sizzling pan.

He put the plate down in front of Slocum with a flourish.

"You see, Mr. Slocum, when we woke up this morning, we did a little exploring, and discovered some other buildings out that way." Harvey pointed to the north, over a short hill. "We found a henhouse and a smokehouse."

"Yeah," Lawrence Stanwell piped in, "and we went looking through what was left of *our* house, and found some plates and cooking things!"

He smiled as if to say, "And there you are!"

"I'll be," Slocum said. He dug into the food, which was excellent. "You see anything else out that way?"

"Well, we looked for the Mexican gentleman Miss Belinda spoke of, but he was nowhere in sight. There were cattle out there, though!"

"Yeah, but there weren't any little doggies!"

Harvey turned and looked at his skinny friend with bewilderment. "What do you mean, there weren't any little doggies?"

"Isn't that what they say? Get along, little doggie?"

Olivier threw up his hands. "I give up." He turned back to Slocum, who was already cleaning his plate. "Anyhow, Mr. Slocum, we found lots of cattle, but not as many as Miss Belinda said there would be. There was a hole in the fence out there, and maybe that's where they went!"

Slocum pondered. "I think we'd better take a

look at that hole, and fix it right away.

"Anything you say, Mr. Slocum."

Still thinking, and slightly worried now, Slocum finished his coffee and got up.

"Let's go right now," he said.

Lawrence and Harvey led him to the hole, which, as Slocum had thought, was man-made. Bordering this section was land owned by Bart Forsen, and Slocum had no doubt that Forsen had been bleeding off Nate Carver's herd while the man was away.

"Give me a hand," Slocum said, hefting up one of the fence posts which had been loosened and tossed aside, and soon the three of them had repaired the fence.

"Good as new," Slocum said. "Now I think we'd better take a look farther up the line here, and make sure there aren't any other breaks."

With Lawrence and Harvey trotting along, and occasionally tripping behind him, Slocum followed the fence for a good half mile before coming upon another break. He scanned the cattle herd behind them, and estimated its size at about half what Helen Belinda had said it was.

"Looks like Mr. Bart Forsen's been up to a lot of no good," Slocum said.

Harvey Olivier pointed to a spot in the near distance, over a series of rolling hills. Slocum saw that it was a farmhouse, just visible.

"Isn't that the place Miss Belinda went to?" Harvey said.

"I imagine it is," Slocum said, waiting patiently while Lawrence Stanwell dropped and then picked up again his end of a post Slocum was attempting to replace in the fence break.

Lawrence dropped his end again, and Slocum gently persuaded him to leave it where it was. He looked confused, then wandered away.

Slocum turned his attention to mending the fence, and was almost done when Lawrence Stanwell called from a spot up the fence line.

"Hey, Mr. Slocum, come here!"

Slocum finished with the final slat, then walked over the short rise to where Lawrence stood beaming next to a mule, which had been tied to the fence.

"It's a horse!" Lawrence said, beaming up at Slocum proudly.

"It's a mule, actually," Slocum said. "And I imagine it belongs to that Mexican fellow who was helping Carver out."

Already knowing in his gut what he would find next, Slocum continued up the fence line until he came to what at first looked like a bundle of rags on the ground.

It was a body, and as Slocum carefully turned it over with the toe of his boot, he saw that it was a small man who looked Mexican. On further examination, Slocum saw that he had been shot in the back.

Lawrence and Harvey stood behind him.

"Oh, dear," Harvey said.

"He's dead, and not too long," Slocum said.

"He was murdered. I know a little bit about this kind of thing, and I'd say a sharpshooter did it, from a good enough distance away. Kind of a cowardly way to murder a man, if you ask me."

At that moment a shot rang out in the near distance.

"Get down!" Slocum shouted, pushing Lawrence and Harvey to the dirt.

Slocum's trained ears measured the next shot, determined that it came from somewhere over across Bart Forsen's property, and that it was not aimed at them but rather at the house where Helen Belinda had gone.

In a moment Slocum was on his feet. "Let's go," he said.

"Where are we going?" Harvey Olivier asked.

Slocum looked at him, suddenly grim.

"We're going to help some ladies who need it," Slocum said. "And we're going to start something that I'm afraid will end badly."

12

Slocum heard more shots, widely spaced, as they headed over to the former Belinda place. Slocum rode on ahead, rifle at the ready, as Lawrence and Olivier ran behind him, keeping their heads down the way Slocum told them. Soon Slocum had left the two dudes in the dust, and pulled up in front of the now-quiet farmhouse on the former Belinda property.

It was quiet, and Slocum didn't like that.

Ready for anything, Slocum dismounted and crept to the front door, which was open.

A line of bullet holes were scattered across the door frame, and on into the house, against a far wall.

"Anybody in here?" Slocum called out.

Still, he was met with silence.

Behind him, through the open doorway, he saw the tiny running figures of Lawrence and Harvey growing in the distance.

Slocum made his way to the hall stairs, and

moved slowly up them, rifle at the ready, steps creaking.

He heard the click of a hammer above him, turned the rifle up with lightning speed, ready to shoot—

"John—thank God it's you!"

Helen Belinda looked down at him, face white with fear but also determination, as she turned her own sawed-off rifle away, putting it down.

"Oh, John, it was horrible. . . ."

In a moment Slocum was up the stairs, catching her as she fainted.

He held her until she came around, as Lawrence and Harvey, breathing like steam trains, came into the front parlor downstairs.

"Anybody home?" Lawrence called idiotically.

"Up here," Slocum said, noticing now that six worried faces had filled the large doorway at the top of the stairs.

"You girls all right?" Slocum asked.

They nodded.

"Nobody hurt?"

"Just Maggie here, a little," one of the girls said, pushing the slightest of them forward to show the long tracing line of a bullet-winging along one arm.

"You'll be all right," Slocum said.

In his arms, Helen Belinda roused and woke.

"Oh, John," she said.

"You're all right now," Slocum said.

"I never even saw who was shooting at us!" Helen said, sitting up on her own.

"I counted the seconds on the early shots," Slocum said. "The reason you didn't see anyone was because he was a half mile away. Safely on the Forsen property. We're dealing with a sharpshooter here."

"But towards the end, just before you got here, we did hear something," Helen went on. "A kind of . . ."

"A hiss," one of the girls in the doorway said. "Like a snake."

Surprised, Slocum turned to Lawrence and Harvey. "Isn't that what you two heard back East, when Nate Carver was killed?"

"That's right," Harvey said. "Just like a snake."

"Well, I'll be," Slocum said. "And all the time I thought you were mistaken."

"Oh, we're never mistaken," Lawrence Stanwell said. "We might always be wrong, but we're never mistaken."

Harvey rolled his eyes.

"Well," Slocum said, turning his attention back to Helen, "the thing to do is get you ladies out of here safely. I take it you were going back to town today anyhow?"

"That's right," Helen said.

"Well, I think you should go now. We'll go with you. Then I think I'll come on back and have a little talk with Mr. Bart Forsen."

Helen put her hand on Slocum's arm. "You don't have to get involved in this because of us, John."

"I'm involved for lots of reasons. You, and them," he said, indicating Harvey and Stanwell, "and because this snake business has me thinking. There was a fellow I crossed paths with a long time ago."

Slocum's attention drifted to the past for a moment, but then he was back in the present.

"Never mind about that now. The important thing is to get you all safe into Parsonage."

Helen nodded.

"All right." She turned to the six still-frightened girls in the doorway. "You know what has to be done. Let's get out of here as soon as we can!"

The six faces retreated, and soon Slocum heard the sounds of packing.

Standing up, Helen Belinda looked around her wistfully.

"This used to be a wonderful house," she said. "When I grew up here, there were nothing but good memories in this place."

Her eyes drifted to a line of bullet holes in the wall at the top of the stairs.

"But that was the past," she said.

Slocum looked at her.

"We'll see what we can do about fixing the present," he said, and then he climbed the stairs to dig a slug out of the line of holes in the wall and pocket it.

13

They were a motley crew, heading out a little while later: Slocum at the lead on his Appaloosa, rifle ready, scanning the Forsen property for signs of the shooter; and in the wagon a half-dressed gaggle of ladies and two dusty Eastern dudes in their midst.

Helen Belinda drove the wagon, her own rifle out and next to her.

But there were no shots fired, and soon they were on the dusty road back into Parsonage, and then in Parsonage itself.

Helen pulled up in front of the saloon, and the ladies piled out of the wagon, leaving Lawrence and Harvey bowing and alone inside. The ladies had regained their humor, and giggled at the galantry of the two dudes.

"Go on in," Helen ordered the ladies. "Tell Sam I'm here and'll be in in a minute."

Dutifully, the ladies trooped off into the saloon.

"I can't thank you enough, John," Helen said. Slocum noticed that she had regained her tough exterior, though they both knew now that it was in many ways a mask.

"Maybe you can," Slocum said, and Helen smiled.

"Maybe I can at that, but now I've got work to do. These girls have to get settled in. And . . ."

She put her hand on his arm.

"I want you to be careful," she said, serious. "I wasn't joking about Bart Forsen. And Sheriff Rowles too. Things are even worse than I thought, now."

"I'll look out for myself," Slocum said.

"You'd better," Helen said. She smiled. "And I'll see what I can do about thanking you soon."

Slocum tipped his hat.

Over Slocum's shoulder, Helen Belinda saw something she didn't like.

"Uh-oh," she said.

Slocum turned to see Sheriff Rowles, a hard look on his face, walking purposefully toward them from the sheriff's office across the street.

Rowles nodded ever so slightly at Helen, then turned his attention immediately to Slocum.

"You're new here," he said, not at all friendly, "and you didn't check in with me when you rode in yesterday. We have a law in Parsonage about strangers passing through here. We like to know who they are and what they want."

"Doesn't seem like much of your business, Sheriff," Slocum said, making his face just as hard as Rowles's.

For emphasis, Slocum slid his hand casually

down toward his cross-draw holster, stopping it a few inches away but making sure that Rowles saw that he was ready for a fight here and now if he wanted it.

Rowles's face reddened with anger. "Listen, mister—"

"It's all right," Helen Belinda said quickly to Rowles. Her voice became friendlier than it had been before. "He's with me, Sheriff. I hired him on to help the new owners of Nate Carver's ranch."

"*You* hired him on?" Rowles asked.

"That's right." She nodded back at Lawrence and Harvey, who smiled dumbly from the back of the wagon. "Those two Eastern dudes there bought Nate Carver's place, and they're friends of mine. Mr. Slocum here will be helping them get on their feet."

Rowles studied Slocum. "Get on their feet, eh?"

"That's right," Slocum said.

Rowles suddenly laughed. "Well, *that's* a good one! Carver's place is ready to blow away in the wind." He pointed at Lawrence and Harvey, who still smiled, and laughed even harder. "And *those* two dandies are going to work that ranch! Ha!"

He stopped laughing, mirth lines still creasing his eyes, and said to Slocum, "Look, stranger, I don't know who you are or where you came from, but if I were you I'd convince those two jokers to sell out to a fellow named Bart Forsen, and quick. Forsen'll give them boys a good price, and they can go back East and spend it on a couple of brains.

One way or the other, Bart'll be wanting that ranch land, and I can tell you from this side of the badge that you'd be doing well to deal with him now. Or . . ."

Realizing that he had gone too far, Sheriff Rowles became quiet.

"Or what, Sheriff?" Slocum asked.

"Never mind," Rowles said.

"Or maybe those two dudes'll get bullets in their backs?"

"Now just wait a minute," Rowles said, reddening in anger again.

Slocum said, "Sheriff, I'd like to report a murder on Nate Carver's old property. Me and the two dudes found the body of a Mexican fellow named Franco this morning. He'd been shot in the back."

Rowles shrugged. "Mexicans're always getting themselves shot in these parts. Bury him if you want, but I can't see as it's any concern of mine. He was probably trespassing anyway."

"Nate Carver hired him before he went East."

"Still, it's no concern of mine," Rowles said.

"How 'bout someone shooting from Bart Forsen's property at Miss Belinda and her girls here with a Sharps .69-caliber?" Slocum took out the slug he had dug out of the wall of Helen Belinda's old house and dropped it into the sheriff's hand. "That's a buffalo hunting rifle, Sheriff."

"I know what it is," Rowles said. He turned to Helen Belinda. "This true?"

"It's true."

"Where were you at the time?"

"At my daddy's old house."

"Then *you* were trespassing. You know that place don't belong to you no more," he said.

Helen Belinda's eyes smoldered. "I know."

"I'll have a talk with Bart about the shooting, though."

"Thank you," Helen said, eyes still burning.

"Since you seem to be Bart Forsen's messenger boy, tell him this," Slocum said. "Tell him those two boys sitting in the wagon there are going to not only work that ranch, but make it a success. Come this time next year they may even make Forsen an offer to buy *his* place."

Rowles blustered with anger.

"You tell Forsen that," Slocum said.

Slocum turned away slightly, knowing Rowles would go for his gun, and before the sheriff had his six-shooter out of his holster Slocum had drawn smoothly across his body and held his own Colt under the lawman's nose.

"You went first for your gun," Slocum said evenly. "Everyone here saw it. I'm going to keep this as friendly as I can, for now. I don't mean to break any laws, and I don't mean to bother you as long as you stay out of my law-abiding business. But remember this," Slocum said, his tone hardening. "If you pull a gun on me again, whether to my front or my back, be prepared to go all the way with it, because I will. That's not a warning, it's just the way things are."

Breathing hard, Rowles said nothing, but eased

his hand away from his gun, leaving it in his holster.

Slocum put his own gun away.

"Like I said, Sheriff, I haven't broken any laws and I don't mean to. Let's just keep it where it is."

From the doorway of the sheriff's office across the street, Slocum saw the barrel of a rifle protruding. He nodded toward it.

Rowles waited a moment, then turned quickly and blurted out, "It's okay, Curly! Put the rifle down!"

"Thank you," Slocum said.

"You're pretty quick, Slocum," Rowles said.

"Only as quick as I have to be," Slocum said. He tipped his hat. "See you, Sheriff."

"I'm sure you will," Rowles said, and with as much dignity as he could muster, he turned and walked back to his office.

"Do you think that was smart, John?" Helen Belinda asked.

"It was the only move to make," Slocum said. "A man like that won't push past his limitations. He knows there's plenty of other places and times to take care of me. He wasn't about to do it out here in front of the shopkeepers unless it was easy. I showed him it wasn't easy. Now we can walk the town without trouble. The trouble'll come out by the Bar B Ranch."

Helen moved suddenly closer to Slocum, real fear coming into her eyes. "You'll be careful, John, won't you?"

Slocum smiled down at her. "Sure I will."

She pressed into him. "I mean real careful. I couldn't bear it if anything happened to you."

"Is that a fact?"

It looked as if Helen Belinda would blush.

She turned quickly away.

"I've got work to do," she said, starting toward the saloon. Suddenly she stopped and turned back. She took Slocum's hand and pressed something into it.

"I meant it about hiring you," she said, and Slocum saw that she had left five dollars in his palm. She nodded back toward Lawrence and Harvey. "They can pay me back when they can. Take the wagon, I don't need it now. I want you to make the Bar B Ranch run again."

Slocum smiled. "All right, Helen, I will."

Still threatening to blush, she turned and hurried off into the saloon, leaving Slocum holding a suddenly hefty poke.

Slocum turned to Lawrence and Harvey.

"Come on, boys," he said, "let's go shopping!"

14

The dry-goods store had Havana cigars, and Slocum treated himself to one out of his own poke. With the money Helen Belinda had given him he bought two bedrolls and a week's stock of food.

Seeing Slocum's Havana, Lawrence Stanwell asked if he could have one too, and Slocum put an extra one on the bill and gave it to him.

"Thanks!" Lawrence said, and went outside to light up.

When Slocum came out with the supplies five minutes later, Lawrence was leaning against the front of the store, looking sick, the lit cigar held limply in his hand.

"Haven't you ever smoked one of them before?" Slocum asked.

"Sure," he said. He demonstrated by lifting the cigar to his mouth and blowing three perfect smoke rings. He smiled at Slocum sickly.

"Then what's the problem?"

Harvey, standing next to him, rolled his eyes.

"After he lit the cigar he put the lit end in his mouth!" he said in exasperation.

"Come on," Slocum said, shaking his head in disbelief. He loaded the back of the wagon, including the two dudes, tied his Appaloosa to the back, and climbed up front.

"Time to go home," he said, snapping the reins.

When they had left Parsonage behind, Harvey Olivier suddenly began to sing, in a beautifuly sweet tenor voice, "My Old Kentucky Home."

Slocum turned around to see Lawrence Stanwell watching his friend with an innocently blank smile on his face.

When Harvey had finished his song, Slocum said, "I've been meaning to ask you something. With that accent of yours, where're you from?"

"Why, the beautiful state of Georgia, of course!" Harvey said.

"You don't say," Slocum said. "I was born there myself."

"Do you miss it, Mr. Slocum?"

"Can't say," Slocum said. "That was a long time ago. Before the War Between the States."

Harvey sighed. "Sometimes I miss Georgia. I think spring is the most beautiful time there, Mr. Slocum. I miss the Cherokee roses blooming, and the brown thrashers singing in the live oaks. I miss the look of peanut and cotton fields too, and especially peach trees."

"It's a beautiful place—what I remember about it," Slocum said.

"Have you been on the road a long time, Mr. Slocum?"

Slocum paused before answering.

"Yep," he said finally.

Harvey sighed again theatrically. "Someday I think I'd like to go back to Georgia," he said.

"Someday I think I'd like to go back too," Slocum said.

"Me three," Lawrence said.

Harvey turned to him. "Why, you've never even been there!"

Lawrence nodded. "That's right."

"So how can you go back?"

"Well, you see, if you miss a place terribly, you can always go back to it."

"But you've never *been* there!"

"But I can always go back, can't I?"

Harvey threw his hands up in frustration. "I give up!"

"Oh, don't do that!" Lawrence said. "If you do that, you won't be able to go back!"

"Mr. Slocum," Harvey said, "please stop the wagon for a moment, so that I can strangle Mr. Stanwell."

"But if you do that, *I* won't be able to go back!" Lawrence cried.

His face screwed up as if he were going to cry, and then he began to sputter, "And I want to go back!"

Slocum broke out in a laugh, and after a moment Harvey Olivier began to laugh also, and soon all three of them were laughing as Slocum moved the wagon toward the Bar B Ranch.

15

But the laughter stopped soon enough when they reached the ranch.

They could see the dark curls of smoke even before they topped the rise giving them a view of the Bar B. When they could see, it was obvious that the collapsed house, which just that morning had held the potential for rebuilding, had been set afire and was now a smoldering heap of ashes.

"So much for salvage," Slocum said, pulling his Winchester from its saddle scabbard and keeping it at the ready.

They took the wagon in a slow turn around the burned wreckage. There was nothing to save; everything had been burned in an almost expert fashion. Someone had even heaved Lawrence and Harvey's lean-to of the night before into the inferno, as well as the makeshift kitchen table and chairs.

"Looks like someone really doesn't want you boys to make a start of it," Slocum said.

Slocum stopped the wagon and climbed down. He checked the Winchester over, then handed it to Harvey Olivier.

"Ever handle one of these?"

Harvey's eyes went wide. "No, sir."

"Well, it's time to learn."

Slocum gave the fat man a short course of instruction, then nodded toward Lawrence. "And I'd keep it away from him if I were you."

"Oh, I will, Mr. Slocum," Harvey said.

Slocum said, "I'm going to check the rest of the property out. I'll check out the immediate surroundings first. What I'd like you two to do is get in front of that smoldering pile of junk with it between you and the Forsen property. This way that sharpshooter can't get at you. Anyone approaching from the front of the Bar B you'll be able to see. I won't be gone long."

"Mr. Slocum?" Lawrence asked.

"What is it?"

"Well, do you think we can still build a home here?"

"I can tell you this," Slocum said, trying to hold his anger at Forsen inside. "No one's going to force you off your own land."

Lawrence smiled weakly, crinkling up his eyes.

Slocum smiled. "Want a cigar?"

"No, thank you," Lawrence said.

Slocum left the two of them cowering in front

of the smoky ashes of their home, and rode off, letting his anger out now that he was alone.

To himself he said, "I think it might be time to visit Mr. Bart Forsen."

16

As Slocum had feared, the rest of the Bar B Ranch was in similar shape to the ranch house.

The henhouse and smokehouse had been reduced to rubble. Whoever had done it had had a good time; everything was beyond repair, and the chickens in the henhouse had been gleefully slaughtered. The bacon in the smokehouse had been stolen.

Slocum rode on, already knowing what he would find on the rest of the property.

There were no longer breaks in the fence—it had simply been eliminated, knocked down flat, every post pulled and tossed aside, the slats chopped to pieces so they couldn't be reused.

And the cattle were gone, lured over to Bart Forsen's land. Slocum could just make out a couple of them with the distinctive B brand on them.

Slocum was mad, but he was also smart, and had the feeling he was being watched even at this second. If he rode off pell-mell across the fence line now toward Forsen's ranch house, he had no doubt

he'd be shot down from a distance. With only his
Colt to protect him, he knew the better course, and
the one most likely to get him face to face with the
cattle baron, was to go through Forsen's front gate
like any other visitor.

One thing to do first, he thought.

Riding to the spot where the Mexican Franco had
been murdered, Slocum dismounted next to the
body. The flies were already starting to get at it.

"Sorry I can't do better, friend," Slocum said,
wishing he had a shovel, but knowing he would
only be able to make a shallow mound of dirt over
the carcass.

At that moment the Mexican's mule topped a
rise and ambled down to where Slocum stood.

"Well, I'll be," Slocum said, finding a saddlebag on the mule containing the Mexican's tools,
among which was a good solid shovel.

Slocum patted the mule, which stood obediently
nearby.

"You were a good friend to this man," Slocum
said, and set about digging a proper grave.

When he had finished, Slocum stood over the
freshly covered ground and removed his hat. Words
might be proper, but of what use were they now?
How many bodies had Slocum stood over in the
span of his years? How many times had he beheld
the dead? What words of comfort could a man like
Slocum say to a dead man?

Slocum said no words of religion, but rather
made the dead man a promise.

"I'll try to straighten this out for you too, Franco," he said.

Slocum patted the mule on the rump, sending him ambling back toward the ruins of the ranch house, where Lawrence and Harvey hopefully would not shoot him.

Then Slocum remounted his Appaloosa and rode off to visit Bart Forsen.

17

Bart Forsen's spread was a grand affair. Slocum
rode miles, sweeping past new fences erected on
properties that had at one time belonged to Forsen's
neighbors, before ever reaching Forsen's original
property itself. Slocum counted five old spreads,
their abandoned ranch houses sitting like ghosts
while Forsen's cattle grazed nearly up to the
porches. In entryways where proud family ranch
signs had once hung, were now simple signs saying, "PROPERTY OF BART FORSEN." The man
truly owned land from horizon to horizon.

Finally Slocum reached Forsen's own ranch
house, after riding under a freshly painted sign on
two huge and tall posts that read in script, "FOR-
SEN RANCH." The brand was an F over a com-
mingled R, also in script, and quite attractive.

As Slocum entered the ranch unmolested he
passed an area where that brand was being newly
applied to a cow that Slocum was sure had held

the brand of Nate Carver's ranch not five minutes before.

"Can I help you, mister?" a voice called out behind Slocum, and now Slocum heard the click of a gun being cocked.

He turned to see one of the branders with a Colt, the other one now cradling a rifle. The Colt was aimed in Slocum's direction.

"John Slocum to see Bart Forsen," Slocum said easily.

"Is that so?" the first brander said.

The one with the rifle grinned. "You got an appointment?"

"No, but since I represent the two men who now own Nate Carver's ranch, I thought he might like to speak to me."

"You come to sell?" the rifleman said, still grinning.

"No," Slocum said simply. "I came to talk."

"Talk to yourself then," the rifle-bearer snapped, his smile disappearing as he held the rifle up closer to using position.

"Now hold on," the one with the Colt said to his friend. "We should check with your father first, Bill."

"Hell with that!" He brandished the rifle. "Get moving, mister!"

Slocum stayed where he was.

Bill, twitching now in anger, held the rifle up to eye level, sighting along it. Slocum's reflexes tightened, ready to dodge a bullet and possibly shoot one himself.

"Bill, what are you doing?" came a hard and very loud voice from the porch of the ranch house.

Slocum turned to see an extremely tall, thin, and weathered-looking old man regarding both him and the others. He looked like a crafty old bird of prey, eyes hooded and cold. He wore no hat, and his open-necked shirt revealed the neck of an old turkey buzzard who had been through a lot of scrapes and meant to last through a lot more.

Bill's face twitched and his breath came out in little gasps.

"Bill!" the old man said, in the most even voice Slocum had ever heard.

Suddenly the young man jerked the rifle down and stood breathing in gasps, face twitching, as if he had been struck by lightning.

"Get back to what you were doing," the old man snapped, and now it was as if Slocum wasn't even there as Bill and his companion returned to branding the cow. Slocum noticed that Bill's breathing returned slowly to normal, and in a moment it was as if nothing had happened.

The old man turned his hooded eyes to Slocum.

"I'm Bart Forsen," he said.

Slocum nodded slowly.

"I'm—"

"I know who you are," Forsen snapped. "Come in."

Without another word, the tall man turned and left Slocum sitting on his horse, leaving the door to the ranch house open behind him.

18

After Slocum had gone, Lawrence Stanley and Harvey Olivier stayed crouched low behind the smoldering pile of what had merely been the collapsed ruins of their ranch house.

"Hey, Harvey, you know what?" Lawrence asked his fat friend.

"What?" Harvey Olivier said, giving Lawrence the kind of expectantly suspicious look he was used to giving in these kinds of situations. Usually at a time like this, it was Lawrence's cue to say something inane.

"I was just thinking," Lawrence said.

"About what?"

"About us. I was thinking maybe we'd be better off where we came from."

Relaxing his suspicion slightly, Harvey said, "Perhaps you're right. It seems we've been in nothing but a jam since we came out West."

His skinny friend gave him a perplexed look.

Harvey said, "Didn't you mean we'd be better off back East?"

"No, where we came from," his friend said blankly. He pointed at the wagon. "There. The seats in the wagon were much more comfortable than the ground here, and we wouldn't have the hard ground under us—"

His hat flew off as Harvey shoved him in consternation.

"You idiot! Didn't you listen to a word Mr. Slocum said? If we had stayed in the wagon we'd be shot!"

Rubbing his fingers up through his hair, Lawrence pointed again at the wagon. "But we'd be much more comfortable."

Harvey gave a groan of impatience, drew back his palm to shove his skinny companion again— but suddenly he froze.

"Did you hear that?" he said.

"Hear what?"

"That noise. Shhh . . ."

He put his finger to his lips, urging Lawrence to be quiet.

Lawrence whispered loudly, "What noise?"

"That!" Harvey whispered fiercely back, and now they both heard it, the sound of whistling, close and getting closer.

"Doesn't sound like a snake!" Lawrence whispered.

"Be quiet!" Harvey said.

The whistling suddenly stopped.

"Now you've done it!" Harvey said. He pushed

his friend and pointed upward. "Stand up and see who it is!"

Lawrence screwed up his face in hurt.

"You stand up!" he whined. "You've got the gun, and . . ."

"Hello?" a voice, very close, said.

Lawrence and Harvey screamed in fright, Harvey fumbling the rifle in his arms, standing and falling as the rifle nearly fell and he barely caught it, holding it pointed backwards at the figure standing over them.

"Now you don't move!" Harvey said.

The figure, short and smiling, wearing a sombrero, pointed at the reversed rifle in Harvey's hands.

"I think you've got it the wrong way to shoot me," he said in a Spanish accent, smiling.

"Anyhow," he continued, "I have no gun myself, so maybe we can be friends?"

He put out his hand.

"I am Victor Herera, brother of Franco Herera, who works here for Mr. Nate Carver!" He smiled.

Suddenly cordial, Harvey laid the rifle down, wiped his hand on his trousers, and held it out, bowing as he shook hands.

"How do you do! I am Mr. Harvey, and this is my friend Mr. Stanwell. And—"

Suddenly he frowned. "Did you say you were Franco's brother?"

"Why yes, is he here?"

"I'm afraid he's . . ."

Victor looked perplexed.

Lawrence drew his finger across his throat.

"He's . . ." Lawrence said, nodding his head in certainty.

Angry, Harvey knocked his friend's hand away from his throat.

"Why did you do that!"

"Well, it's true, isn't it?"

"Yes, but . . ."

Crestfallen, Victor Herera said, "My brother has been killed?"

Harvey reached out to pat his shoulder. "I'm afraid so. Mr. Slocum, who is helping us here, found him yesterday. Mr. Slocum said he'd been shot in the back. But don't worry—Mr. Slocum will take care of it!"

Staring into space, Victor said, "I cannot believe my brother is dead! We were both promised work here by Mr. Carver, and Franco went ahead to help. And now . . ."

His face became angry. "Who is the man who did this thing? I will kill the man who did this thing to my brother!"

"Now, now," Harvey Olivier said, continuing to pat Victor's shoulder.

"Where is Mr. Carver?" Victor said in a rage. "How do I know *you* did not kill my brother?"

"Mr. Carver is . . ."

Again Lawrence drew his finger across his throat.

Victor's eyes grew large with anger. "How do I know *you* did not kill Mr. Carver?"

Lawrence smiled inanely. "*We* own this place now!"

"I will kill you!" Victor Herera said. He marched away from them toward a mule which stood close by; in a saddle scabbard was a rifle, and Victor made to draw it out.

"Mr. Herera, please!" Harvey pleaded. "Mr. Stanwell didn't mean—"

"Sure I did!" Lawrence said indignantly. He smiled at Victor. "*We* own this ranch now!"

Snorting in fury, Victor Herera drew his rifle from its scabbard as Harvey Olivier pushed at his uncomprehending skinny friend and cried, "Run!"

"But—!"

"Run, Lawrence! Run for your life!"

Lawrence looked at Victor Herera, now drawing a bead on him, and now comprehension dawned, and he cried out in fear, his legs pumping underneath as he ran after his friend around the smoldering pile of ranch rubble.

A shot rang out overhead, and they heard Herera cursing at them, cocking the rifle again.

"I will kill you!"

"Now look what you've done!" Harvey said as they ran.

Another shot rang out, whizzing over their heads.

"Keep running!" Harvey Olivier shouted.

19

At the Forsen Ranch, Slocum followed Bart Forsen into the entryway of his ranch house.

Inside it was as grand as Slocum expected it to be. The wide hall was walled in dark wood, mounted with hunter's trophies, elk and deer heads. The hall led into a spacious living area dominated by a huge stone fireplace. The stone looked imported.

Forsen, stopping by the mantle, caught Slocum eyeing the stone.

"New England granite. Brought in from New Hampshire," Forsen said. His tone held neither pride nor pleasure in it, but rather an almost defensive taunting. As if he were saying, "It's here, it's mine, what are you going to do about it?"

Slocum nodded slightly as Forsen poured himself a drink from a decanter on the mantle. He didn't offer Slocum one.

Forsen turned to Slocum, eyes hooded, mouth grim, and took a quick sip from the whiskey.

He even drinks like a bird, Slocum thought.

"So, Mr. Slocum," Forsen said, without preliminaries and without a trace of friendliness, "how can I make you go away?"

Slocum waited for a moment without answering. Then he said, "I wasn't planning on going away, Mr. Forsen. Not until I like things in this part of the country anyway."

"You don't like Parsonage?" Forsen asked, unsmiling.

"Not the way it is," Slocum said.

"What about those two fools who own the Carver Ranch?" Forsen asked. "You think they're worth getting killed for?"

"I wasn't planning on getting killed, Mr. Forsen. I thought maybe we could work this out before the killing starts."

For the first time, a tiny, grim smile crossed Forsen's lips. But the rest of his face still look like a stone carving of a cold watchful hawk.

"Been a while since I met one like you," Forsen said. "In the war, weren't you?"

Slocum nodded.

"But that was a long time ago," Slocum said.

Forsen nodded.

"I'm not one to reminisce myself," he said. "Living through that war was just as hard as living now—for our side."

"We were talking about the present, Mr. Forsen."

Forsen nodded. Again he smiled tightly.

"It's just that I admire you, Mr. Slocum. And to

be honest, I fear you a little bit. Not what you can do to me, but what you can do to what I have here."

"What you have here is a tin-pot dictatorship," Slocum said. "You own everything in sight: the law, the town, the land. And you don't want anything to disturb it."

Forsen nodded slowly. "That's right, Mr. Slocum. I don't want anything to disturb it. Certainly not you. It would be much simpler for me if you just . . . went away. I'd be willing to pay you to do that."

"Because you realize if I stay around there'll be trouble."

"That's right, Mr. Slocum. I'm not only ruthless but I'm smart."

"And you realize that if there's trouble, that twitchy son of yours out there is liable to be in the middle of it, and get himself killed along with a lot of other men."

"Along with you, Mr. Slocum."

"That's a matter for debate, Forsen."

Forsen turned to refill his drink, and after taking another quick, birdlike sip, he sighed. "I'm willing to pay you a lot."

"And what about the two dudes who own Carver's place? And Helen Belinda, and the others whose ranches you stole?"

Forsen looked down at his drink for a moment, then slowly placed it on the mantle. When he looked up at Slocum his eyes were unblinking and hard back under his hooded brows.

"The two fools I'd be willing to give an almost fair price to, as part of your deal. But the others . . ." He shrugged. "What's done I won't undo."

"No deal, Forsen."

"I think we both knew that's the way this discussion would end, Mr. Slocum."

Slocum heard the merest hint of breath, a kind of low hiss, from Forsen's right. He had just enough time to react before a panel in the wood next to the stone of the fireplace burst open, revealing a secret hiding place, and a gun muzzle flashed.

But Slocum was already dropping and rolling, pulling his Colt from its cross-draw holster and firing at the secret spot.

The room became a blaze of gunfire. Slocum pulled off four wild shots and counted five and then six from his opponent. Slocum was already moving for the door as he heard Forsen behind him shouting, "Reload and get him, you idiot! Isn't that what I'm paying you for?"

The hissing became loud and angry, and now Slocum was out through the door, firing off two more shots and then jumping from the porch to his waiting Appaloosa. Behind him he heard frantic movement and Forsen shouting, but by the time the next six shots were fired he was already out the gate, under the huge Forsen Ranch sign and past the startled branders, who had dropped their tools to gape at the scene in wonder.

Keeping low, Slocum avoided all six shots, and

knew he would have at least a minute or two before his opponent could retrieve his Sharps rifle, set up the tripod, and attempt a long-range shot at him. In the meantime, the two branders had taken up arms and were firing at him wildly, which bothered Slocum not at all.

Right now he had only one gunman on his mind: the man who had rushed at him from the secret hole in the wall, and who now would try a desperate shot from a buffalo hunter's gun.

The shooter had been a coward—albeit a deadly one—when Slocum had first come across him, and he would no doubt still be a deadly coward now.

"So, Jim Crain," Slocum thought grimly, "we meet again."

20

Slocum was well out of range of even Jim Crain's Sharps rifle when he heard a shot.

At first he thought Crain had taken a try at him in desperation, but his ear told him that the shot— followed now by another—had come from the Bar B Ranch.

His Colt reloaded and ready, Slocum cut through the broken fence, and was approaching the smoldering ruins of the Bar B's ranch house when a wild-eyed figure tore across his line of vision and headed out over empty country.

The figure suddenly reined up on his mule, turned toward the pile of smoking ruins, held a fist to the sky, and shouted, "I swear by God I shall kill you both! I will return!"

Puzzled now, Slocum headed in toward the wreckage as the rider turned, not seeing Slocum, and rode off, shouting oaths.

"Hey, dudes!" Slocum called out, dismounting from his Appaloosa. The grounds were eerily quiet, and nearby was the mule Slocum had sent back to the ranch house.

"Mr. Slocum, is that you?" came Lawrence Stanwell's muffled British voice from somewhere close by.

At first Slocum thought the voice was coming from the mule.

"Where are you, boys?" Slocum called.

"Is it safe?" came the muffled tenor of Harvey Olivier's voice.

"Sure, come on out!"

With a groan, Harvey Olivier stood up not five feet from where Slocum stood, in the midst of the ashy wreckage.

Both figures stood up, covered in black soot, looking as forlorn as can be.

"What happened?" Slocum asked.

"That Mexican fellow mistook us for Franco's killers," Harvey said pitifully, "and swore he was going to kill us."

"And he will, too," Lawrence added, nodding his head in certainty. "Until we're d-e-d."

"That's d-e-a-d!" Harvey shouted in exasperation.

"Whatever," Lawrence said.

"Come on out of there and clean yourselves up," Slocum said. "I'll straighten that Mexican fellow out when I get a chance. We've got more important problems."

"Oh?" said Harvey with interest.

Lawrence said, "What could be more important than being d-e-d?"

Harvey looked at him murderously, but gave up and said nothing.

"Just this," Slocum said. "Things are worse here than I thought. That fellow Bart Forsen not only owns everything around here, he's at the point where he can do whatever he wants and get away with it. What they need here is outside law, but I don't think that's going to happen, and it's not anything I'd want anyway. I don't think Miss Belinda and her girls are safe either."

Harvey's face showed alarm. "Can we help them?"

"We have to," Slocum said. "And anyway, we need them. What we have to do is fortify a base camp here, and get ready for a siege. And I don't think it'll be long before it starts. Forsen'll get some men from town, and be ready to drive us out before you know it. Just like I thought, he's got a killer working for him, sharpshooter by the name of Jim Crain. He's bad business, cold as a snake—in fact, he's the man you heard when Nate Carver was killed. He's got a lisp, a thing with his teeth, and when he gets excited it sounds like he's hissing. They used to call him Snake Crain back in Fort Worth, where I first came across him. And he's sneaky—he popped out of a secret hole in the wall back at Forsen's place. What we need to do is guard the perimeter of the ranch, make sure Crain can't set up his Sharps rifle within range of our compound."

"Then what, Mr. Slocum?" Harvey Olivier asked innocently.

Slocum sighed. "Then we try not to get killed."

21

Putting himself in the mind of a man like Forsen, Slocum thought they'd have at least till the next day to set up. Forsen would reason he cold attack at leisure—after all, he no doubt believed he had all the cards in his favor. He had the men, the resources, the law on his side; so, Forsen would figure, he had time on his side too.

But this was where Slocum meant to beat him. And that meant getting Helen Belinda and her crew out to the Bar B as soon as possible.

When Lawrence and Harvey were spruced up as much as possible, they set out toward Parsonage. Slocum put the two dudes in the wagon, while he scouted out away from it, careful to keep as much flatland between himself and the horizon as possible. Though it was more likely that Snake Crain was back at Forsen's ranch drinking whiskey to celebrate chasing Slocum off, it was possible the marksman could have set up his tripod on one of the surrounding hills and be waiting to put Slocum and his companions in his sights.

But there was no Snake Crain evident, and soon Slocum was able to rejoin the wagon as Parsonage grew close in the near distance.

And between them and the town a figure stumbled toward them, a girl in tattered rags.

"Mr. Slocum!" cried Harvey Olivier in alarm as the figure collapsed before them.

Harvey stopped the wagon as Slocum dismounted. Harvey was the first to the girl, bending down to cradle her head.

She opened her eyes and smiled weakly.

"I know you. . . ." she said, smiling weakly. "You're funny. . . ." she said, and passed out.

"It's one of the girls from Miss Belinda's place!" Harvey said.

Slocum produced his flask from his saddlebag, and held it to the girl's lips.

She came to and looked up at Slocum.

"Helen . . ."

Her eyes fluttered closed again, and once more Slocum pressed whiskey to her lips.

This time she was stronger.

"Sheriff Rowles . . . took Helen . . ."

"What about the rest of the girls?" Slocum asked.

"Sheriff's deputy Curly . . . beat us . . ."

"Where are the rest of them?"

"In the saloon . . . hiding . . . I . . ."

Slocum waited.

"I ran away. . . ." she said, and drifted down to unconsciousness.

Slocum put his flask away, and helped Harvey Olivier lift the girl to the back of the wagon.

Quickly, Slocum checked his Winchester, and made sure his Colt was filled with lead.

His eyes had filled with cold fire.

"Let's go," he said.

22

Slocum left the wagon with the unconscious girl in it guarded by Lawrence just inside town, behind the livery stable. Slocum checked all through the stable and found it empty, coming back to arm Lawrence with a sledgehammer.

"If anyone comes near you, wave this at them and growl," he said.

Harvey Olivier insisted on coming with Slocum, and Slocum, after arguing, finally relented and gave him the rifle.

"Know which end of this to point?" he said.

"Yes, sir," Harvey said, though Slocum knew for sure he'd be useless in a fight.

They made their way into town.

Parsonage was eerily quiet. A few whirls of dust twirled down the street; somewhere a shutter banged on its window frame, unlatched and creaking. It was as if the town had gone into hibernation.

It hadn't, of course. Slocum knew that behind every window was a scared face, a shopkeeper with a family to worry about, the kind of man who could not afford to stand up to a Bart Forsen. It was an old story but a familiar one to Slocum; the part of the story he didn't like was that possibly behind one or two of those windows, or up on a roof, was one of Forsen's supporters or toadies with a rifle, ready to start shooting when Slocum and his fat companion stepped out into daylight.

So they stayed in shadow, Slocum pushing Harvey back when they came to each window or doorway as he checked it over.

Soon they were at the saloon doors, which creaked slightly on their hinges in the breeze.

"Come in when I tell you," Slocum said to Harvey, noting that the fat man had already managed to turn the rifle around so that he would be pointing it in the wrong direction if he had to use it.

Without another word, Slocum ducked into the saloon, moving one of the swinging doors smoothly aside to slide inside the building.

The main room was empty. But cigar and quirly smoke still curled from ashtrays at a nearby poker table, and a row of drinks stood waiting on the counter of the bar.

Slocum slid over to the bar and looked behind it, expecting to see at least the bartender still in attendance.

The back of the bar was empty.

Slocum made a motion to Harvey outside. When Harvey came in nervously, Slocum gestured to him to move over toward the stairs, and then followed.

"Watch my back," Slocum whispered.

"All right, Mr. Slocum," Harvey said nervously.

Slocum grabbed the Winchester and turned it around. "And hold this the right way," he said.

"Yes, sir."

Slocum moved up the stairs.

At the top, sprawled on the floor, was the body of what must have been the bartender. His apron was flowered with a crimson-red hole where he had been shot.

Down the row of doors, Slocum heard a sound.

He moved to the particular door, listened, and heard a snuffling sound.

Six-gun ready to work, Slocum kicked in the door.

There was a gasp from inside.

And there, huddled in the corner, were the rest of Helen Belinda's girls, frightened and wide-eyed but otherwise unhurt.

"Oh, Mr. Slocum!" one of them wailed.

"Tell me what happened."

The wailing one pointed with a shaking finger at the door.

"The sheriff and his deputy came and tried to make us leave! Helen argued, and then Fred, the bartender, took her side." Her eyes grew wide and scared with remembrance. "Then Curly shot Fred, and left him for dead! And . . ."

"What happened to Helen?"

"The sheriff . . ."

Slocum waited while she sobbed and sucked in a breath.

"Sheriff Rowles took Miss Belinda away!"

"Do you have any idea where he might have taken her?"

The girl trembled and shook her head.

One of the others said in a shaking voice, "He said something about a 'hiding place.' He was laughing when he told Curly that."

"You have any idea what that might mean?"

The girl shook her head.

Slocum looked down at the frightened girl, at all the frightened girls, and said, "Don't worry. You'll be all right now."

Slocum called down to Harvey Olivier, who appeared a moment later in the doorway. He had managed to turn the rifle around again.

Slocum sat him down on a chair in front of the frightened girls. He laid the rifle in Harvey's lap, put Harvey's shaking finger on the trigger, and pointed at the doorway.

"If anybody comes through there, shoot," he said.

Slocum walked to the door.

"But where are you going, Mr. Slocum?" Harvey Olivier called.

"I'm going to find Helen Belinda."

23

Slocum knew he didn't have much time. Bart Forsen might already be assembling his own men to attack the Bar B Ranch, and here in town, Slocum had to assume he would meet nothing but enemies. Already, what little he had in the way of defense was spread out and almost useless. Harvey Olivier might get one shot off if attacked, but it would all be over after that. And as for Lawrence Stanwell, guarding the wagon . . .

Slocum shook his head.

But there was more immediate danger to worry about. The sheriff's office was across the street, and Slocum had a fair idea he'd be shot at on the way there.

Peering out through the saloon's swinging doors, he spied a figure in the half-open window of the sheriff's office, gun drawn.

Slocum sprinted for the rear of the saloon and pushed his way into the storeroom, where he found four patrons cowering on the floor, continuing their card game.

Slocum held his gun on them.

"We ain't got no quarrel with you, mister!" a grizzled gent said, holding his hand of cards up in protection and fear.

Slocum said, "I don't think two pair'll be enough," and moved past them as the grizzled man swore and threw his cards down.

His companions laughed.

The back door was blocked by a few cases of whiskey, and Slocum moved them aside. Suddenly one of the cardplayers was there, helping him. Slocum recognized him as the owner of the dry-goods store.

"There's a short alley, but you don't want to use that," the man said. He was old and tired-looking, but his eyes were fiery. "One of Forsen's men was in town helping Rowles with something, and they posted him in the back. What you want to do is go into the storeroom of my place next door, then out the back door there."

His eyes were measuring Slocum.

"There aren't many of us that like what Bart Forsen's done, mister," he said. "Most of us he stole from. But he just wore us down. It comes to a real fight, though, I think you'd find some help in Parsonage."

"It's good to hear that," Slocum said, " 'cause I might need it."

The man nodded.

"Any chance you could go upstairs and help my fat friend out?"

"Sure," the man said. "Four of us'll do it." He called back to his mates, "We can set up the card game upstairs, right, boys?"

They grumbled their consent.

"Fred was a friend of ours," the man said. "Best bartender we ever had in this town. And Curly gunned him down like a dog. It ain't right."

"Just be sure you call out that I sent you before you go upstairs," Slocum said. "He's got a rifle up there and I told him to use it."

"We'll do that, mister."

"Name's Slocum."

The old man held his hand out. "I'm Matt Grierson. We've been waiting a long time for a man like you to show up in this town. What Forsen's done ain't right. What he forced Helen Belinda to become ain't right either. After he stole her daddy's place she didn't have much choice. Nowhere to go, nothing to do. And I've got to tell you that Rowles has had his eye on her for a long time. Be seeing you, Mr. Slocum. And be careful." He gave a slim smile. "I noticed you like those Havana cigars I've got. There's an open box in the storeroom. Help yourself."

"Thanks," Slocum said, and then he opened the door and slipped out into the alley.

24

The old man Grierson had been right; there was a man posted at the end of the alley. Slocum could just see him, sitting on a barrel, hat slouched down over his face, sleeping.

Slocum crossed the alley quietly and eased open the door on the other side. He found himself in the back of the dry-goods store. It was dimly lit, but he was able to make out the piles of boxes and skeins of yarn.

And there was the open box of Havanas Grierson had mentioned.

Slocum took a handful and put them in his pocket.

"Least this job has *some* rewards to it," he said.

The back door had a key set in it, and Slocum turned it, opened the door, and stepped out.

The back of the dry-goods store jutted out further than the saloon next door, and Slocum was invisible to the man waiting at the end of the alley there. Slocum moved away to the next alley, which brought him out a good distance from the sheriff's office. With the angle of the buildings, Slocum doubted the man waiting in the office would see him when he crossed the street.

He dashed across, into another alley, and moved around to the back of the buildings there.

He made his way carefully down to the rear of the sheriff's office. The bars of the holding cells were visible there; a slop bucket lay tilted at a drying angle against the wall, next to the only door, which was ajar.

Colt ready, Slocum moved the door fully open, peering into glooming jail-cell dimness.

There was a short hallway between the cells, which then opened out into the main office beyond.

Slocum could just see the left side of whoever was at the window, a nervous fellow who moved back and forth, into and out of sight, his left hand holding a pistol as his head bobbed around the window, searching the outside.

The man turned enough to the left so that Slocum could see his profile.

Colt still ready for action, Slocum moved up past the cells, two on the right and two on the left. His eyes were intent on the man at the window.

Suddenly there was a sound from the second cell on the left.

There was somebody in it.

"Hey, Curly!" the man inside shouted. Slocum saw a bleary-eyed man rush at him, clutching the bars.

Slocum drew back from the surprise, and at that moment the man turned from the window, startled also, and aimed at Slocum.

Two deadly smoking lines of fire crossed, as Slocum and the man at the window both shot at the same time.

The shot of the man at the window went wide, pinging off one of the bars in the bleary-eyed man's cell, making him dive for cover, shouting.

But Slocum's shot found its mark, and the man at the window slumped to the floor, and then fell dead.

"Jeez, you got him!" the bleary-eyed man in the cell said. "You got Curly! What a shot!"

Slocum walked cautiously to the front room and checked the body.

"Boy, that was some shooting, mister!"

Slocum walked back to the cell. "What are you in for?"

The man made a drinking motion with his hand. "Little too much last night. Fred had to kick me out of the saloon."

"Fred's dead."

"You don't say. You know, I ain't surprised. He and Curly had a terrible row last night. Curly the one who shot 'im?"

"From what I've heard."

The drunk shook his head.

"Too bad. Fred was a good bartender too."

Slocum went to Curly's body and removed the ring of keys on his belt.

"You gonna let me go, mister?" the drunk called.

"That depends on how good your eyes and ears are."

"Oh, I see and hear real good, mister."

"You have any idea where Sheriff Rowles went?"

The man was looking beyond Slocum, to Rowles's desk, which stood near the front door.

"Something you need in that desk?" Slocum asked.

"My ears and eyes get even sharper after I have a drink," the man said.

Slocum went to the desk and began to pull drawers out.

"Upper left-hand side," the man said eagerly.

Slocum pulled out that drawer, and pulled out the whiskey bottle that was in it.

"Real thirsty," the man said.

Slocum brought him the bottle, uncorked it, and let the man down a finger or two of whiskey.

"That's enough for now," Slocum said, taking the bottle back.

The man looked at the bottle, then at the key ring.

"You gonna let me go *and* give me the bottle?"

"You drive a hard bargain," Slocum said.

"I know where Rowles is," the man said, lowering his voice.

"Tell me," Slocum said.

"You unlock me and let me have the whiskey?"

"Sure."

The man lowered his voice again. "You gotta promise not to tell anyone where you heard it."

"Tell me," Slocum said, tiring of the games.

The man indicated the bottle, licking his lips, and Slocum gave him the bottle for one more drink.

Slocum yanked the bottle back in the middle of the man's guzzling.

The man looked at the bottle longingly, then lowered his voice and leaned toward Slocum.

"There's an old shack, two miles east of town," the man said. "Used to be a squatter's shack. Rowles took her there."

The man looked at the bottle, but Slocum was waiting for more.

"Will he be alone?" Slocum said.

The drunk looked at the bottle with longing.

"He sure will," he said. "He goes there with his lady friends sometimes. I happen to know that he's had it bad for Miss Belinda for a long time. I don't think he was going to take no for an answer this time, if you follow me."

Slocum already had the cell door open, had thrust the bottle into the man's arms, and was on his way out the door before the man could react.

"Gee, thanks, mister!" the man called.

But Slocum, his eyes hard and his mind set, didn't hear.

25

"I've been waiting a long time for this," Rowles said.

The trip to the shack, for which Sheriff Rowles had bound Helen Belinda hand and foot and then thrown her over a horse like a sack of meal, had been bad enough, but Helen knew that worse was coming. A man like Rowles was bad enough sober, but the sheriff had been drinking, which made him even more unpredictable and reckless.

"We've known each other a long time, Ted," Helen said, looking up at him from the straw mattress where he had thrown her.

"That's right," Rowles said drunkenly, "and I've wanted you a long time."

"I told you that was never going to happen," Helen said, trying to keep her voice calm. "I told you that as long as you worked for a man like Bart Forsen—"

"The hell with Bart Forsen!" Rowles said, waving his arm drunkenly in dismissal. "I don't work for Forsen. I work for *me*."

"That's not true and you know it. You helped Forsen drive all those ranchers out. You helped Forsen drive my father out."

Rowles started to protest, then picked his bottle up from the floor instead and took a drink.

"All I wanted was . . . to be big," he said.

Unable to control her anger, Helen said, "And are you happy now, Ted?"

"No!" he said. In his drunken state, his face took on a confused look. "All I wanted was to impress you."

"Impress me?" Helen laughed. "By destroying my father and all his neighbors? By forcing me into the kind of work I do now?"

"You didn't have to do that," Rowles said. "You could have . . ."

"Married you?"

"Sure."

Helen laughed. "I told you I'd rather be a madam than your wife, and I meant it."

Rowles snarled in anger, then took another drink.

"Well," he said, "I'll have you now anyway."

Helen laughed derisively. "Like this? You call yourself a man?"

"Sure I'm a man," he said. A sudden, cunning smile came onto his face. He bent down over her. "And I'll prove it to you now."

He laughed, pulling at her blouse, and ripped it away, exposing her naked breasts. Helen screamed, trying to move away, but she was bound too tightly, and soon he had stripped her clothing away, leaving her naked but defiant below him.

"You're not a man," she spat. "You're nothing but an animal."

Rowles took another drink, then put the bottle down. He reached down to loosen his gunbelt.

"We'll see who's a man," he said.

There came a loud crash behind him, and the door flew open.

Rowles turned, grabbing for his six-shooter, which slipped into his hand as his gunbelt fell away.

He raised the gun to fire.

Slocum stood in the doorway, Colt ready, and got off three shots before Rowles had fired once.

The lawmen slumped to the ground, dead before he hit, a look of surprise on his drunken, shocked face.

Slocum walked past the body, holstering his gun, and bent down to untie Helen Belinda.

"Did he . . . ?" Slocum asked gently.

"No," Helen said. "But he had it in mind."

When Slocum had loosened her bonds, she threw her arms around him, holding him tight.

"Oh, John, I don't know what he would have done to me!"

"Well, you're safe now," Slocum said.

She pulled back from him, looked into his eyes, and smiled coyly. "We don't have to let this naked condition of mine go unused, John."

Slocum felt the manhood rise in him, but held it down.

"I'm afraid we do, Helen," he said. "There's no time now."

While she was dressing, he explained the situation at the Bar B Ranch to her, and what they had to do.

"My girls are safe?" Helen asked.

"For now. But we have to get everyone to the ranch, and be ready for Forsen when he comes. Nothing's going to stop him now."

"We'll do everything we can to help," Helen said.

Slocum smiled. "That's what I wanted to hear."

Outside the shack, Slocum helped Helen up onto Rowles's horse, then mounted his own Appaloosa.

Leaving the shack behind, Helen Belinda looked at Slocum and said, smiling, "But there'll be time for us later, won't there, John?"

"We'll make time," Slocum said.

26

When Slocum and Helen Belinda arrived back in Parsonage, things were pretty much the way Slocum had left them. Harvey Olivier still guarded the girls in the room on the second floor of the saloon, though by now the shopkeeper Matt Grierson and his cardplaying buddies had joined them.

Grierson said, "This fat oaf tried to shoot me when I came in!" He pointed at Harvey. "Even after I told him that you'd sent us!"

Harvey Olivier looked sheepish, but then Matt Grierson laughed. "Good thing he was holding the wrong end of the rifle toward me, or someone might have gotten hurt!"

Slocum moved everyone downstairs and into the street, and went to fetch Lawrence Stanwell, who had fallen asleep in front seat of the wagon he was supposedly guarding.

The unconscious girl he had been watching over was awake, brandishing the sledgehammer Slocum had given Lawrence, while Lawrence slept contentedly, a smile on his face, with his head in her lap.

When Slocum woke him up he yawned, stretched, and said, "Oh, hello, Mr. Slocum!"

Shaking his head in disbelief, Slocum brought the wagon out of the alley into the street to join the others.

Matt Grierson, the shopkeeper, had loaded one of his own wagons down with supplies and food and sat waiting to go.

"Thanks," Slocum said. Turning to the others he said, "We're going to go in a caravan to the Bar B Ranch," Slocum said. "I'll scout ahead, and I want you to all stay together. Keep your weapons ready. When we get to the ranch we'll organize work details. I don't know how much time we have—"

Unexpectantly, Ben Forsen, along with his son and six more armed men, rode out of the alley next to the saloon.

Glancing upward, Slocum now saw four other shooters on the roofs of nearby buildings, pointing their rifles down toward them.

"Looks like you've got us, Forsen," Slocum said, his hand itching to go after his own Colt. But he knew that if he did he might get Forsen and maybe one other—but the battle would be over right there.

Forsen, a tall sprectral figure in the saddle, turned his hooded eyes and unsmiling mouth on Slocum.

"You were a fellow fighter in the Southern

struggle for independence," he said. "I could wipe
the lot of you out right here, but honor would not
let me do that. So I propose to let you return to
your ranch, and make your preparations. I vow not
to attack before the morning after next."

Slocum noted the slight glistening in Forsen's
eye.

"You figure on re-enacting Bull Run, Forsen?"

The glistening transformed itself to the slightest
of smiles.

"Something like that, Mr. Slocum. In any event,
that is what I promise. Except . . ."

Forsen made a slight motion with his right hand,
and from somewhere above and behind Slocum a
shot sounded.

Matt Grierson fell dead from his wagon, shot
through the heart.

In the near distance, Slocum heard the eerie hissing sound that followed the sharpshooter Jim Crain
around like a plague.

"You call that fair?" Slocum asked.

Without blinking, Forsen said, "Mr. Grierson
was a traitor. His place was in town. That is also
the place for his three companions."

Forsen turned his hooded dark eyes on Grierson's three cardplaying friends, who scrambled out
of the back of Grierson's wagon and into the
swinging doors of the saloon.

"Outside of that," Forsen said, "you are free to
go. You can even take the supplies the late Mr.
Grierson was kind enough to give you."

Slocum locked stares with Bart Forsen.

"We don't have a choice, Forsen, but I want you to remember this. Jim Crain is going to pay for what he just did, and so are you."

Forsen turned his mount around and began to ride off.

"We'll see, Mr. Slocum. The morning after next."

His back to Slocum, Forsen rode off, his small army following.

27

"We've got a lot of work to do," Slocum said. While Helen Belinda took control of one wagon, Slocum put Harvey Olivier in charge of the other.

After Forsen had left, Matt Grierson's three friends came out.

"We took a vote, and we still want to come with you, Mr. Slocum," they said.

Slocum pondered, then shook his head.

"Sorry, boys, but you'd never make it to the Bar B Ranch. I know Jim Crain, and he'll be out there somewhere, waiting to pick you off. I could sure use you, but I've got no use for you dead."

Forlornly, the three trudged back into the saloon.

"All right," Slocum said, "let's move out."

It was a dejected band that moved out of Parsonage, and a dejected band that arrived at the Bar B Ranch. Night was almost falling.

"Think we can make a fire?" Helen Belinda said.

Slocum pondered, then nodded.

"Call me a fool, but I believe Forsen will keep his word. It would have been all over back in town if he'd wanted it otherwise. He's got a twisted kind of logic in his head, but when he said he won't come at us until day after tomorrow, he meant it. We can build a fire."

Soon there was a meal cooking, which everyone wolfed down with abandon. The warmth of hot beans in Slocum's belly felt good, as did the taste of hot coffee. Once again Lawrence and Harvey played at being cooks, to the giggling delight of Helen Belinda's girls.

"You dudes are all right," Helen said.

"Thank you, ma'am," Lawrence said, blushing.

The stars came out, and Helen bedded her companions down on blankets from Matt Grierson's wagon. Lawrence and Harvey slept nearby, on the opposite side of the dwindling fire, with the Mexican Franco's mule, which had waited for them, standing nearby.

Slocum drew himself a last cup of coffee, stood, and stretched.

"Where you going, John?" Helen asked.

Slocum pointed out toward the perimeter of their little camp.

"I've got a little scouting to do. Even though I believe Forsen won't go back on his word, I still can't completely trust him."

"Will you sleep at all?"

Slocum shrugged. "If I can. I'll make camp out there somewhere, if things look safe."

"Be careful, John."

Slocum smiled at her. "I will."

He ambled off into the growing darkness.

Slocum made a bedroll up away from the others, then went scouting.

There wasn't much moon, so even if Jim Crain got any ideas of his own, there wasn't enough light to work by.

Crain, of course, was the one Slocum didn't trust. Bart Forsen might give his word, but Jim Crain, being a coward and scoundrel, had no word to give. The best Slocum could hope for was that Forsen had the sharpshooter on a short enough chain. With a man like Crain, you could never be sure.

But things were quiet enough. Slocum wandered over to where the chicken coop and smokehouse had been. Kicking around in the embers, he discovered a few unburned boards that they could make use of. With a little ingenuity, they could make some kind of defense.

Up the line away from the smokehouse, the broken fence line stretched away into the night.

After two hours of wandering and thinking, Slocum, convinced there was nothing more to do this night, returned to his little camp.

He sensed movement a good distance away. Drawing his Colt smoothly across his body, he edged forward, ready. The area around his camp was empty, but a lone figure was in the camp itself.

As Slocum drew closer he saw that the figure was hiding in his bedroll.

He knew who it was, but kept the Colt out to make sure. Silent as a cat he crept up on the bedroll, edged the top back—

Helen Belinda gasped, then stared up at him with wide eyes. She was naked as a jaybird, and began to shiver.

"Lord, John Slocum, you scared me. Now get in here and get me warm again."

Slocum put his Colt down nearby, and in a moment was out of his own clothes and in the bedroll face to face with the beautiful madam.

"I couldn't let the opportunity pass, John. Kiss me."

Slocum kissed her, and felt her body melt around him like butter. Her hand snaked down to find his manhood, already stiffening, and suddenly she was guiding him into her wet recesses, impatient.

"Oh, John!" she gasped, thrusting herself down around him so that he was buried down to the root of his stiffened shaft inside her.

"Oh, John, fill me up!" she whispered fiercely.

She prodded him onto his back and, still holding him tight and wet inside, began to move on top of him. As she worked on his rock-hard member, driving herself down on him and then pulling up so that Slocum's hot tip was just inside her, Slocum watched her creamy breasts bounce and her nipples lengthen and harden. Her chill was gone; she was a slickly oiled machine, moving on top of him like a love animal, her long sweat-soaked body primed and tight.

"Oh, John! John!"

She threw the bedroll back completely, and now dug her nails into Slocum's buttocks as she filled herself up with him. Slocum felt himself begin to fill with the cum juice she so desired; when he did let go, he feared he would blow her to pieces.

But this was what she wanted, what she begged for; her dry open mouth rasped in pure pleasure as she pistoned Slocum into her, feeling him grow even harder and larger inside—

"Now, John!" she gasped, unable to hold out any longer.

And she came with him, their simultaneous explosions nearly shaking the ground beneath them. Their muffled cries of release were nearly exceeded by the sound of their bursting loins: Slocum's cum burst into her, filled her cavity to overflow, roared down and out around Slocum's cock, and covered their two nether areas in a hot white flow. It felt as if a hot river had burst from its dam and covered them with love.

When it was finally over, Helen brought the bedroll back over them and collapsed onto Slocum's chest.

"Oh, John, that was . . ."

Before she could finish, she was asleep.

"Wonderful," Slocum finished for her, smiling at her sleeping form. He had a feeling that everything she had saved had been put into this one time, that with all the tension and fear of the day, all the uncertainty of what would come next, there would be no repeat this night.

He was wrong, and just as he was nodding off himself, she awoke and, laughing, groped again for Slocum's love rod.

"Ma'am, you sure are something," Slocum said.

"So are you, John," Helen said, and as she mounted him again, still wet below from their last encounter, she gasped and repeated, "So are you!"

This time, she let Slocum do some of the work, and when they were done, with results similar to their first tussle, she held onto him and said, "I'm scared about what's going to happen, John."

"Don't be," Slocum said. "We'll do what we can."

"Just hold me, John," she said.

Slocum held her, and soon she was asleep again, this time for the night.

"We'll do what we can. . . ." Slocum whispered, repeating it for his own benefit.

And so Slocum lay there with the sleeping woman, his own eyes open, listening, waiting for what the next day would bring.

28

The next day came all too soon.

Helen awoke at dawn, and dressed just as Slocum was beginning to nod off. He felt her bend down and kiss him, and when he awoke it was two hours later and he was the last to get going.

Lawrence and Harvey had breakfast waiting for him, though, and after eating, Slocum felt as if he could conquer the world. He had almost as big a job to do in one day, and knew it was about time to do it.

To his surprise, he saw Matt Grierson's three cardplaying friends helping Lawrence and Harvey clean the dishes.

"They snuck in on a wagon last night, under cover of darkness," Helen Belinda explained. "Said they'd rather die quick here than die slow in Parsonage."

Slocum tipped his hat to the trio.

"Glad you boys came," he said.

"We'll do whatever we can," said the spokes-

man, an unshaven fellow with a firm eye. "That
fellow Forsen took land from all of us, and we're
tired of living the way we do." He held out his
hand for Slocum to shake. "I'm Bentine, and these
other two are Corben and Soames."

Slocum shook their hands, then turned his attention to Bentine again.

Slocum said, "This is important. You have any
idea how many men Forsen'll come at us with?"

Bentine scratched his chin, but Soames, a small
fellow who looked as if he'd be at home behind a
plow, said immediately, "Figure on up to two
dozen. He's got almost that many that live in his
bunkhouse, and before we left Parsonage we
checked around and found that he'd roped in a few
more from town. He only took the ones he knew
would fight for him."

Slocum pondered. "Two dozen . . ."

Bentine said, "And you can figure that half of
them are good shots. Besides that sharpshooter,
he's got a handful who know how to use a gun in
a fight. A couple of them he's used before to bush-
whack ranchers. That's how he started this thing.
He's always surrounded himself with good men."

"What about his son?"

"Bill?" Bentine laughed. "Couldn't shoot the
side of a hill if you pointed him at it. But he's a
hothead, and liable to do anything."

"I figured that," Slocum said. Once again Slocum pondered. "Any of you boys do war service?"

Corben, lean and quiet, suddenly came to life.
"I rode two years with Phil Sheridan."

Slocum gave a slow smile. "Yankee, eh?"

"That's right," Corben said, unsmiling.

"Well, Yankee," Slocum said, continuing to smile himself, "we can use you. We can use you all." He widened his attention to include the entire group.

"I don't need to tell you that our lives depend on what we do. Bart Forsen means to wipe you all out and own Parsonage lock, stock, and barrel. But one thing I've noticed in taking Forsen's measure is that he's arrogant. He doesn't think he can lose. And that's how we'll beat him. The only thing that worries me is our lack of firepower."

Now it was Corben's turn to smile.

"I can help with that," he said. He brought Slocum to the wagon he and his companions had ridden in on, and with Soames's and Bentine's help threw back the tarp covering the bed.

"Well, I'll be," Slocum said in wonder.

There, besides more supplies and food, was a clutch of perhaps twenty Winchester rifles, along with enough ammunition to last a month.

Corben said, "You should of counted on good luck when you got a Yankee on your side. I've been collecting these things for years, storing them away for a day like this."

"Doesn't hurt that he's the town gunsmith either," Bentine said, and they all laughed.

"And I can tell you a few things about Bart Forsen too," Corben went on. "He was a Confederate captain when he fought against Sheridan, and I still remember the tactics he used. I bet he'll use the same ones against you.''

"Well, I'll be,'' Slocum said, slapping Corben on the back, the plan that was forming in his mind suddenly solidifying. Now he had all the firepower and information he'd ever need.

29

Out at the far reaches of the Bar B Ranch, Lawrence Stanwell and Harvey Olivier were doing their part, though they barely had any idea what they were doing.

"What do you think Mr. Slocum has in mind?" Harvey asked his skinny friend, who lifted one end of a fence slat, brought it forward two inches toward the newly erected post, then put it down. He walked to the other end of the slat, picked it up, and moved it forward two inches before laying it down to walk back to the other end.

At his friend's question he shrugged, and bent down to pick up the other end of the slat again.

Harvey watched him, frowning, and then asked, "By the way, what are you doing?"

Lawrence stood up and looked at his friend blandly. "I'm doing what Mr. Slocum said."

"He told us to put the fence back up—why are you moving each end a tiny bit at a time?"

Lawrence's face filled with confusion. "Didn't he say to work slow?"

"No, he didn't!" Sudden realization turned Harvey's puzzled visage into one of outrage. "Why, you idiot! Mr. Slocum said to put the fence back up to slow down the enemy!"

"Oh," said Lawrence. "I thought he said, 'Work slow, and we'll knock down the enemy.' "

Harvey threw his hands up. "What am I going to do with you!"

"Well I just—"

"Give me that!" Harvey said, grabbing the fence slat from his friend's hand and thrusting it into its post in a smooth motion.

"There—is that too much for you to handle? Now let's move up the hill to the next section."

Harvey turned to the mule, which they had brought with them, and which held their lunch as well as a few tools on its back. The animal regarded them unblinkingly with its dark eyes.

Harvey laughed fussily, and spoke to the mule. "Now, Gladys, we're going to the top of the hill!"

Still laughing, he pointed up the rise to the top.

The mule showed no reaction, but gazed straight ahead.

Harvey walked a few paces, then turned back, urging the animal to follow.

"Gladys?"

The mule stood still.

"Maybe you have to push her," Lawrence piped up.

He made a pushing motion with his two hands.

Harvey stared at him. "Well?"

"Well what?" Lawrence said.

Harvey's face reddened. "Get behind the mule and push!"

Blanching at the onslaught, Lawrence moved behind the mule and called out to his friend. "Now?" he asked.

"No, tomorrow morning!" Harvey shot back acidly.

In a moment his companion was standing beside him.

"What are you doing?" Harvey asked.

Lawrence explained, "You said to wait until tomorrow—"

Harvey pushed him violently. "Get back behind that mule and push!"

Rubbing his arm where Harvey had pushed him, Lawrence walked back behind the mule, muttering, "Well you needn't be so loud about it."

Harvey stood in front of the mule and took hold of its bridle.

"All right, push!" he called back.

While his friend pushed from the rear, Harvey pulled from front.

"Come on, Gladys!" Harvey urged. "Come on!"

"Are we there yet?" Lawrence called from the back.

"No, we're not there yet! We haven't moved an inch!"

Straining with effort, Harvey shouted, "Come on, Gladys, let's go!"

The mule stood easily rigid, barely straining against their efforts, its black eyes devoid of emotion.

"Oh, this isn't working!" Harvey said. He let go of the bridle and shouted back, "Stop pushing!"

"What?"

"I said stop pushing!"

In defeat, Harvey sat down on the ground and held his face in his hands. In a moment his skinny friend had joined him.

Suddenly the mule sat down, making a row of three.

Not seeing the mule, Harvey said forlornly, "I just don't know what to do. We'll never get that mule up the hill."

The mule stood suddenly, Lawrence and Harvey still not noticing, and walked slowly up the hill to stand at the crest.

"Maybe if we ask Gladys nicely," Lawrence suggested.

"What makes you think *that* will work?" Harvey said. He shook his head sadly. "We're failures."

"I still say we should ask nicely. Or maybe use a stick. You know what they say: a stick in time saves nine."

"That's a *stitch* in time saves nine! What am I going to do with you?"

"I was merely saying what my grandmother always told me: A stitch in time is a penny earned."

"I give up!"

Harvey looked up and saw the mule at the top

of the hill. It didn't register at first, and he looked
away, suddenly turning back again to stare at
Gladys, who looked down at them with equanimity.

"Look!" Harvey said.

Lawrence, still busy mixing proverbs, looked up
at the animal, waved, and smiled, then went back
to what he was doing.

"And if you take a penny, and stitch it, you'll
have earned a stitch and—"

"Will you look!" Harvey shouted.

Lawrence looked back up at the mule, and this
time the sight registered.

"You see—it worked!" he said happily.

"What do you mean, it worked?"

"Well, like I said, if you take a penny and . . ."

Harvey glared at his friend until the skinny fellow stopped talking.

"Come on!" Harvey said, and followed the
mule to the top of the hill, where it waited patiently
for them.

30

Three hours later Lawrence and Harvey were still mending fences when a lone figure rode toward them.

"It must be Mr. Slocum!" Harvey said. "Let's keep working so that when he gets here he'll be proud of us!"

They ignored the figure, and began to whistle, putting up fence posts and sliding slats into them. The figure was almost upon them before they heard an angry shout.

"You two!" came the angry voice of Victor Herera, dead Franco's brother. "I vowed I would kill you, and now I will!"

Lawrence and Harvey looked around to see the Mexican bearing down on them on his mule, eyes wild, swinging a machete over his head.

Harvey shouted, "Run!"

The two of them scrambled away as the Mexican, with a shout, rode madly toward them. Holding their hats, they ran down the hill, throwing up a cloud of dust behind them.

The mule Gladys trotted leisurely behind.

Lawrence whined, "Harvey, what are we going to do! I don't want to die! I don't want to—"

"Just shut up and run!" Harvey shouted.

Gladys had stopped, and now as Victor Herrera charged over the hill, he was unaware of the mule standing in his path and his own animal bored straight into it.

With a shout, Herrera was thrown from his mount, flew over Gladys, and lay on the ground, stunned.

Harvey and Lawrence stopped to watch, and Harvey began to laugh.

Shaking his head to clear his wits, Victor vowed, "Still I will kill you!"

"Keep running, Lawrence!" Harvey said, losing his humor and turning to flee again.

Once more, they kicked up a trail of dust as Victor Herrera remounted what he thought was his mule.

But it was Gladys, and she calmly sat down with him in the saddle.

Face turning red, Victor threw his hands up in anger.

"I will not be stopped!" he shouted.

Lawrence and Harvey, still running, now saw another figure riding toward them.

While they ran, Lawrence screwed up his face and whined, "Oh, Harvey, do you think he has another brother?"

"I hope not!" Harvey shouted back.

The figure drew closer, and now, behind them, Victor Herrera, cursing to the heavens, got off of Gladys and mounted his own mule.

But his mule and Gladys had now become friends, and Victor's mule refused to move as it gazed into the sitting mule's eyes.

Victor began to tear at his hair.

"I will be avenged!"

He smacked his mule on the flank, and after a moment the animal broke eye contact and Victor, retrieving his machete, climbed on the mount's back and kicked it into action.

"Onward to their deaths!"

Shouting anew in alarm, Lawrence and Harvey ran even faster, now caught between Victor behind them, closing the distance quickly, and the rider in front, who drew yet closer.

"Run this way, Lawrence!" Harvey shouted, turning to the right.

Both Victor and now the new rider turned toward them, Victor closing the distance quickly, machete held overhead for a blow—

"Close your eyes and it won't hurt!" Harvey shouted.

Lawrence closed his eyes as he ran, and waited for the fast-approaching Mexican to strike.

Suddenly a shot rang out, and Victor Herrera gave a shout of surprise.

Stopping in their tracks, Lawrence and Harvey squatted, eyes closed, waiting to die.

Nothing happened.

Cautiously, Harvey opened one eye, and then another.

Victer Herrera sat nearby on his mule, nursing his hand, the machete on the ground nearby.

"What in hell is going on here?" a familiar voice said.

Lawrence opened his eyes too, to see John Slocum, just holstering his Colt and dismounting from his Appaloosa.

"I will kill them with my hands!" Victor vowed, jumping from his mule and charging the two dudes.

Slocum stood in front of the Mexican, holding him tight.

"What is all this?" Slocum bellowed.

"That's the man we told you about!" Harvey said, standing back away from the Mexican, who sought to grab at his neck.

"Yeah, that's Franco's brother!"

Slocum looked down at the angry Mexican. "You think these two bumblers killed your brother?"

"I have vowed to heaven I will kill them for this crime!"

"Only trouble is," Slocum said, "they didn't do it."

Slocum then explained their situation to the Mexican.

The anger drained from the man's face.

"Then I will be your ally forever, and help you fight these men!" Victor Herrera said.

Suddenly he bolted from Slocum's grasp and took Lawrence and Harvey in a bear hug.

"And these two men will be as my brothers, and I will love them to my death!"

Lawrence and Harvey looked sheepish.

Lawrence said, "Does that mean you're not going to kill us?"

Harvey merely groaned.

31

Victor Herrera helped Lawrence and Harvey finish mending the fence, and then they all returned to the camp.

Great change had taken place. Lawrence and Harvey were surprised to see that the pile of rubble that had been the ranch house had been pushed into a long, high wall. To either side of it, the wagons at their disposal had been turned on their sides to provide a shooters' barricade.

Also, recoverable wood from the other structures such as the chicken coop and smokehouse had been hauled to the site to construct more barricades.

In all, a crude circle had been formed, providing a primitive fort.

"Do you think it'll work, Mr. Slocum?" Harvey asked.

"It's worked well enough for the U.S. Cavalry over the past twenty years during Indian attacks," Slocum said. "We've got plenty of rifles, and we'll space them out. I've taught the girls how to load, so there'll always be a loaded weapon ready to use. I've also got a few other tricks up my sleeve," he added.

Harvey and Lawrence waited for him to tell them what they were, but Slocum just smiled and said, "Never mind."

"Can't you tell us anything?" Harvey asked.

"Let's just say I took a page from Jim Crain's book," Slocum said.

"Dinner!" Helen Belinda called out, and they all went to eat.

It was a feast of sorts. Bentine and Corben and Soames had brought plenty of supplies, including fresh game, flour, and canned goods.

Lawrence and Harvey couldn't remember the last time they had eaten this well. After the meal, Lawrence lay holding his stomach with one hand and picking at his teeth with a bone.

"You know, Harvey, I could get used to this," he said.

Harvey looked up at the stars just beginning to dot the darkening sky and said, "So could I, Lawrence."

"You think we'll ever get our doggies back?" Lawrence's eyes grew warmly blank. "You know, I could see myself in our new house, sitting by the fire on a cold winter's night, surrounded by doggies."

In exasperation his friend said, "Don't you know by now that doggies are cows!"

Indignantly, Lawrence said, "Of course I know

that!'' The warm look came back to his eyes. "But
I'd let the cows in the house when it was cold,
because they'd be cold, and all the doggies—I
mean, cows—would sit around the fire."

In disgust, Harvey got up and walked away.

He found John Slocum standing by himself, gazing off over the chest-high wall toward Bart Forsen's property.

"Do you think we'll win, Mr. Slocum?" Harvey
said respectfully.

Slocum said, "To tell you the truth, Harvey, I
don't know. I've done everything I could to give
us a chance, but . . ."

"Yes, Mr. Slocum?"

Slocum said, "I can't help thinking I got you all
into this mess. Forsen's a bully, but I went out there
and provoked him. I made it personal with him.
Now he's taking it out on everyone here."

"That's not true!" Harvey said indignantly.
"Why, without you, Mr. Slocum, we wouldn't
have had a chance! That sharpshooter would have
picked us off like"—he made a motion with his
dainty fingers, as if flicking something—"peas
from a plate! And he's already done wrong to Miss
Belinda, and Mr. Corben and his friends, and
everyone else in this town! Why, Mr. Slocum,
you're our hero!"

Slocum looked at him and smiled grimly.
"Well," he said, "tomorrow we all get to be heroes."

He walked away, found a break in the wall, and

headed out to his own camp at the perimeter, where he would spend the night on watch.

"Maybe tomorrow," he said, "we'll all be dead heroes."

32

Slocum stood facing the Forsen property, reflectively smoking one of his precious Havana cigars, when he felt someone coming up behind him.

His Colt lay nearby, but he knew who it was, and knew whose warm fingers moved over his shoulders to massage his neck.

"Thinking, John?" Helen Belinda said.

"Yep."

"You think too much," she said with a low laugh.

"Yep."

She pulled him around to face her.

"Stop thinking," she said.

"I was hoping you'd come out here," he said.

"Oh," she said, laughing, "I'll come all right."

In a moment the animal that was in John Slocum took over. He moved above her, pulling aside her robe to reveal her creamy long body beneath him. Her dark hair framed her open and waiting face. For a moment he just looked at her beautiful body.

"Aren't you going to kiss me?" she breathed, moving her belly up to push against his middle.

"Oh, I'll do more than that," Slocum said.

The time for thinking and reflection was over.

In a moment Slocum was out of his duds, and suspending himself over her. As he kissed her she took his hardening penis in her two hands, covering its length with her fingers and then moving gently down to cup his balls.

"I want you to fill me up, John," she breathed.

She opened herself, and then took the root of his shaft in one hand and guided it into her already wet insides.

She clamped around him, and felt him slide in, long and hard and ready for work.

And work he did. Slocum became a love piston, driving her to gasp and beg, and then pulling nearly all the way out only to drive home again. The stars turned above them as their love machine turned into higher gear. The sweat covered them like a blanket, and now Helen turned on her belly and let him mount her from behind. On all fours she began to rock like a bucking filly, holding his dick tight and wet inside with her love muscle, wanting to scream out in satisfaction as Slocum became harder still and even more engorged. Soon she would let him give her what she wanted, an explosion of creamy whiteness that would fill her like a hot fire.

"Now, John! Fill me now!"

Slocum gave a mighty thrust, at the same time letting his love gun fire deep within her.

Moaning in ecstasy, Helen rammed her butt end

back against Slocum's forward push, feeling the mighty hot spurts from his hard red member fire off one, two, three. She counted eight blasts, before Slocum grabbed her legs and drove even deeper, letting off one final engorged eruption that completely filled her with his juice and sent her flying forward, taking Slocum nearly out of her as her own volley began to fire.

Slocum followed her forward, driving back in to take her orgasms in riding stride as his whiteness drove out and away from her love hollow to soak both of their middles.

"John!" she shouted one final time, covering her mouth with her hand to keep the others from hearing. A mighty convulsion coursed through her and then she collapsed onto her belly, feeling Slocum slip expertly out of her to rest the still-hot shaft of his softening dick in the wettened crevise of her ass as he covered her with his hot body and whispered into her ear.

"Happy?"

Unable to speak, she nodded, smiling.

Finally she was able to whisper, "I know it'll never be that good with anyone again."

And then, as she drifted off to sleep, feeling Slocum's softening warm penis like the stroking finger of a friend on her lower back, she felt him cover the two of them with his blanket against the night's encroaching chill. Then she heard him whisper, as much to himself as to her, "I just hope we get the chance to try."

33

Unlike Slocum, the next morning came all too soon.

Helen Belinda rose, still naked, to find that John had gone. The sun was just pushing up on the eastern horizon, and as she dressed she saw Slocum outlined against it, studying the far reaches of the property.

"I don't think Forsen'll wait," Slocum said. "I think he'll come as soon as there's enough light."

"Shouldn't you get the others up then?" Helen asked, snuggling herself next to him.

"Already have," Slocum said. "An hour ago. By now they should all be in position."

In the coming light, Helen studied the nearby wall that Slocum had built. She counted only her girls within the perimeter.

"But where—?"

"The others are where I told them to be," was all that Slocum said.

He looked down at her and smiled.

"Time for you to get there with the girls," he said. "I'll be along soon."

Still puzzled as to what he had in mind, Helen approached the wall and went inside to help.

Lighting what he found to be his last Havana, Slocum mounted his Appaloosa and took a short ride. He found Bentine, Corben, and Soames where he had told them to be, as well as the Mexican, Victor Herera, who, Slocum had a feeling, would turn out to be a lucky bonus.

The only ones who hadn't followed his instructions were Lawrence and Harvey—but then, Slocum had figured on that, had made sure they were in the place that looked to be farthest from the action, and had given them the least to do.

"Why aren't you two in that trench we built yesterday?" Slocum growled, after easily sneaking up on the two bumblers as they argued with each other.

"You get in first!" Harvey insisted.

His skinny friend adamantly shook his head. "No, *you* get in first!"

They turned to see Slocum not two feet away.

"Oh, hello, Mr. Slocum," Harvey said, then turned back to yell at his friend before turning to Slocum again suddenly in surprise.

He looked at Slocum sheepishly.

"Didn't I tell you to be in that dugout by dawn?" Slocum said sternly.

Lawrence screwed up his face, pointed at Harvey, and began to cry. "But I'm afraid if I get in first, he'll squash me when he gets in!"

"That's ridiculous!" Harvey shouted.

Slocum said to Lawrence, "Get in the hole."

"But—" Lawrence whined.

"Get in."

Shrugging and still crying, Lawrence climbed down into the dugout.

"Now you," Slocum said.

"Yes, Mr. Slocum," Harvey said.

As he turned to climb down into the hole, he tripped, shouting, and fell into the trench, on top of his friend.

"You see, I told you!" Lawrence shouted triumphantly.

"Idiots," Slocum said to himself.

Two heads rose up above the line of the ground. Lawrence was smiling as if he had won a prize, the bump on his head already forming.

"Now, do you remember what I told you?" Slocum said.

"Yeah," Lawrence said. "You told us we should act like two toads in a hole."

"Something like that," Slocum said. "What you have to do more than anything is be quiet. And if you see anything or hear anything, you give a whistle."

Lawrence whistled expertly.

"That's the way," Slocum said.

Slocum turned his Appaloosa to ride off.

"Oh, Mr. Slocum?" Harvey called timidly.

Slocum looked back. "What is it?"

"Well, sir, don't you think we'd be better off with some sort of weapon? A rifle or such?"

Slocum shook his head and smiled. "I can't think of anything that'd be less useful to you. Just do what I said."

Slocum rode off, leaving the two men looking at one another.

"You think he knows what he's talking about?" Lawrence asked.

"Of course he knows what he's talking about! Didn't you hear him yesterday? He said he gave us the most important job of all! We have to give the signal that starts the battle!"

"You mean it can't start unless we give the signal?"

"Naturally!" Harvey said.

"Then why don't we just not give the signal," Lawrence said, "and there won't be a battle! And then everyone can go home, and no one will fight, and . . ."

His friend looked at him as if he had lost his mind.

"Sometimes I wonder," Harvey said.

"But if we don't give the signal, then—"

"Shut up and do something," Harvey said.

Lawrence began to play with his fingers, interlocking them and then turning the two middle fingers so that they stuck out at opposite side of his palms while he wiggled them.

Lawrence smiled at his cleverness, then tried to unlock his fingers and found that he couldn't.

"What are you doing?!" Harvey said, exasperated.

"Well, you told me to do something."

"I mean do what Mr. Slocum told us to! Not play with your fingers!"

Lawrence smiled inanely, then looked down at his fingers, hopelessly tangled.

He thrust his hands away, and pretended to cock his ear to listen for signs of approach.

All the while, out of Harvey's sight, he struggled with his fingers, trying to untangle them.

Getting angry, he pulled at his fingers, trying to pry them apart, and knocked into Harvey, who was watching with his head above the hole, swiveling his head to listen this way and that.

With a shout, Harvey was knocked aside, his head disappearing into the hole.

When he rose again, his face was covered in dirt. "What are you doing!"

Lawrence held up his hands for inspection.

Groaning with impatience, Harvey smacked at Lawrence's two hands.

They immediately untangled.

Mystified, Lawrence stared down at his freed fingers, then slowly wiggled the fingers, now unencumbered.

He smiled. "Thanks!"

"Ohhh-ohhhhh!" Harvey groaned, knocking Lawrence away from him.

Lawrence fell down, and when he stood up again his fingers were once more tangled together.

He looked down at them with incomprehension.

"Say, Harvey?" he said timorously.

"What is it now!"

Lawrence held up his hands for inspection.

Eyes growing large with anger, Harvey pushed his friend down again.

When Lawrence got up, his fingers were free.

Harvey took his friend by the shoulders and sat him down carefully in a corner of the trench. "Now sit there, and don't do anything!"

"But—"

"Don't do anything!"

"Can I have something to eat? You know, all this waiting makes me hungry, and I'd just as soon—"

"Yes!" Harvey exploded. "Have something to eat! But leave me alone!"

"All right," Lawrence said, talking to himself. "You know I was just trying to help, and . . ."

Totally exasperated, Harvey put his head above the hole again, looking to the heavens for help in dealing with his skinny friend, help that he knew by now would not come.

34

After a while, Harvey Olivier became very proud of himself for doing his job.

Finally, his skinny friend had stopped talking. Lawrence was off in his corner eating something or other, and noisily, but Harvey was able to completely ignore his skinny friend because he, at least, was doing his job.

His head just visible above the hole they were in, Harvey looked this way and that, ears cocked to hear the slightest sound.

The sun was well up now, and Harvey could see to the farthest reaches of the horizon, toward Bart Forsen's property. Between him and the mended fence was little to see—a few scraggly cottonwood trees and a line of churned ground that looked like a prairie dog had been at work.

Suddenly, Harvey thought he heard something— a sound that he had associated with trouble before.

A hissing sound.

"Lawrence!" he hissed in a whisper. "Did you hear that?"

From the far reaches of the hole, Lawrence looked up dumbly. "Hmmm?" He smiled.

"Did you hear that hissing sound?"

"Yes, I did."

"Well, what do you think it could be?"

"Well, it could be a snake, or it could be . . ."

Suddenly Lawrence's face was transformed into a mask of fear.

"Oh, Harvey, it could be that Crain fellow! Ohhhhh!"

Harvey made a sound for Lawrence to be quiet. "Don't say anything! Just whistle!"

"Ohhhhhhh!"

"Shhhhh! Whistle! Like Mr. Slocum told you to!"

Not four feet in front of Harvey's eyes, the ground began to churn as something, still hissing, made its way to the surface.

Something man-sized.

"Ohhhh, Lawrence!" Harvey said, unmindful now of the need to be quiet. "Whistle!"

Lawrence held up the packet of dry crackers he had been eating. "Ohhhhh, I can't!"

He tried to blow sound through his lips, but only a line of cracker crumbs came out.

The ground began to churn, showing a human arm tunneling out now, with a long rifle clutched in its hand.

"Lawrence, whistle!"

Lawrence blew and blew, only spewing cracker crumbs out.

The tunneling arm grew into the form of a man, who drew himself slowly out of his burrowed hole, smiling evily, holding his Sharps rifle up admiringly, as if he couldn't wait to use it.

He hissed when he spoke.

"Hello, boys," he said, laughing evily.

35

Back inside the circle of the man-made wall, Slocum was startled by the sound of a whistle off to the left.

"That was Soames, out by the chicken coop," he said. "Get ready."

The whistle came again, and now a line of men rose over the hill, riding toward them.

Slocum said, "Remember what I said!"

Bart Forsen's men were spread out, just the way Slocum had hoped. He counted ten.

Quickly he moved to a spot in front of them and shouldered his rifle. At his feet were two more Winchesters; the girls and Helen Belinda were spread out in a circle around the wall, waiting.

In shouting distance, Forsen stopped his men and said, "Last chance, Slocum! Come out now and you can leave, along with all your people! All I want is the land!"

"You think he means that?" one of the girls said, fear creeping into her voice.

"He'd slaughter us as we left," Slocum said. "It's already too late and he knows it. I'd wager he has a few more men stationed by the entrance to the ranch, and they'd pick us off like cherries from a tree."

"Slocum, I'm waiting!"

Forsen was desperately trying to see over the wall, spreading his men farther out to either side of him.

"All right, Slocum—get ready to die!"

Forsen made a motion with his hands, and Slocum was pleased to see that he did just as expected, and pushed his men out to either side of him, preparing to throw them around the circle like Apaches attacking a cavalry troop.

"He's doing just what Corben said he would," Slocum said. He allowed himself a brief smile. "I think we've got him."

Whooping like a Confederate captain, Forsen yelled, "Let's get 'em, boys!"

Whooping like Rebels, the split line charged at the wall, circling around it.

"Fire!" Slocum shouted.

To either side of him, Helen Belinda and her girls began to pull off shots. Slocum saw one man fall immediately, even before he had made his first careful shot, and looked admiringly over at Helen to see that she was already taking a bead on another of Forsen's men.

Aiming carefully, Slocum brought one of Forsen's ranch hands into his sights and shot him off his horse. Immediately he turned to another and downed him.

Already, three of Forsen's men were down.

But this wouldn't last; Slocum knew that the strength of Forsen's attack was that once his men had began to circle past each other and attain their speed, they would be hard targets, and as they drew closer they would be able to see over the wall and pick off the defenders.

Forsen knew it too, and as Slocum missed with a shot at the cattle baron he saw a smile of triumph grow on the man's face.

"Keep at 'em, boys!" he shouted.

"Let me get Slocum, Dad!" Forsen's son suddenly shouted, rearing up.

"No! Keep riding like I told you boy!"

Ignoring his father, the boy aimed his horse at the wall, meaning to jump it.

Slocum took careful aim and shot the man from his horse.

"No!" Forsen shouted.

As he passed his dead son, his face flushed red and he screamed, "I'll kill you myself, Slocum!"

The noose drew tighter as the riders closed in on the wall, riding low and fast.

Now Slocum gave a shrill whistle of his own.

With a whoop of their own, Bentine, Corben, and Soames rode over the hill from the area of the chicken coop and smokehouse.

Now Slocum's secret weapons went into action, driving straight at the raiders and scattering their circle. As one man's horse reared up in confusion,

Slocum got off a perfect shot and downed its rider;
to his right, one of Helen Belinda's girls pegged a
lucky shot and downed another.

Suddenly Bart Forsen only had two men left, and
they were scattering.

Two shots from Bentine and Soames, and those
men went down, leaving only Forsen, dazed but
still angry, still on his horse.

"Remember Phil Sheridan, Forsen?" Corben
shouted in triumph.

Suddenly Forsen bolted, lying low.

Two other men of his, who had been in ambush
at the gate, came charging over the hill, but met a
fusillade of fire and went down.

Forsen suddenly reared up, surveyed the damage
with bare comprehension, and held up his rifle.

"I'm not through yet, Slocum!" he shouted in
rage.

Spurring his horse, he tore off away from them,
in the direction of where Lawrence and Harvey lay
in their hole.

And now, to his horror, Slocum heard the weak
shrill of a whistle, and realized that the sharpshoot-
ing, cowardly killer Jim Crain had not been in Forsen's raiding party.

36

Frozen in fear, Harvey Olivier watched as Jim Crain, still half in the hole, slowly brought the long bore of his Sharps rifle around to point directly between his eyes.

"Anything to say, fat boy?" Crain hissed, laughing.

"Yes—*help*!" Harvey said, snapping out of his frozen state. To his friend he yelled, "Quick, Lawrence, whistle!"

Still, a stream of cracker crumbs came out of the skinny man's mouth as he tried helplessly to call for assistance.

"Good-bye, fat boy," Crain said.

Still hissing a laugh, Crain pulled the trigger of his weapon.

There was a *whoomph*, and only a blot of dirt powdered out from the end of the rifle.

"Damn!" Crain hissed. "Must have got clogged in the tunnel!"

"Good!" Harvey said, and suddenly regained

his mobility. He turned and pulled his friend up, pushing him out of the hole.

Lawrence complied, still trying to whistle, and now off in the distance came the sound of rifle shots.

Crain laughed. "That'll be your friends dying, fat boy," he said, trying to pull himself out of the hole and suddenly finding that he was stuck.

"What the—" he hissed angrily, throwing the rifle down to try to yank himself up.

Lawrence stood up and began to walk over to him.

"Can I help?" he asked.

"What are you doing!" Harvey shouted. "Don't help him, help me!"

"Well, I was only trying to be nice."

As Crain cursed, trying to loosen himself from the collapsed tunnel, Harvey motioned Lawrence over and held his hand out.

Lawrence took Harvey's hand, and now a race developed to see who would get out of his hole first, Harvey or the sharpshooter.

Crain hissed, "When I get out of here, I'll blow you full of holes!"

"Ohhhh, Lawrence, please hurry!" Harvey said in agitation, as his skinny friend tried unsuccessfully to pull him out. His hand slipped, and Lawrence fell back into the struggling Crain, who hissed at him wildly, trying to grab at him.

"I'll eat your liver for breakfast, skinny boy!"

Whining, Lawrence slapped at Crain's hands and

moved back away from him, falling into the hole beside the still-struggling Harvey.

"Ohh, get out!" Get out!" Harvey cried.

Harvey once again pushed his friend out of the hole, and the race continued as Lawrence tried to pull his fat friend out after him before Crain loosened himself.

"I'll eat both your livers!" Crain hissed madly, spittle flying from his mouth.

Crain's lower body sudden loosened in the hole. "Ha!" he cried.

"Lawrence, please hurry!" Harvey begged.

Suddenly Lawrence let his friend drop back into the hole as he was halfway out, and tried once again to whistle.

Cracker crumbs came out.

"Get me out of here!" Harvey implored, and once again Lawrence pulled at his friend.

This time, Harvey nearly made it all the way out before Lawrence let go of him.

"What are you doing!" Harvey shouted.

Lawrence, his mind on other things, stood up and blew through his lips.

A weak whistle, followed by a strong one, came out.

Lawrence smiled.

"There!" he said.

Crain, cursing, was nearly out of his hole.

"Get me out of here!" Harvey implored. "Get me out of here or he'll kill us!"

Lawrence's smile evaporated.

"Ohhhhh!" he cried, pulling with sudden power

as his fat friend was finally able to crawl over the lip of the hole.

From over the near hill a figure rode into view, face flushed in anger.

"It's Bart Forsen!" Harvey cried.

37

"Ohhh!" Lawrence whined, starting to run this way and that. "What are we going to do!"

Crain, cursing and angry now, had abandoned trying to get out of the hole and was cleaning the barrel of his gun.

"Crain!" Forsen shouted angrily.

"Shut up, Forsen!" Crain shouted back. "It was you who made me dig this damn hole!"

In anger, Forsen aimed his rifle at Crain, but the sharpshooter had cleaned and loaded and drawn a bead on the riding man.

Before Forsen could fire, a blast from Crain's rifle sent him falling dead from his horse.

"And now you two . . ." Crain hissed, eyes still mad with coward's fire, turning to Lawrence and Harvey.

"Run, Lawrence, run!" Harvey implored, and the two men set off, bumping into one another, falling down, then, still shouting in consternation and fear, getting up again to set off in different directions.

Suddenly, the dirt around Crain's middle loosened, and he stepped out of his hole.

"This'll be easier than I thought," he hissed, laughing, as he dusted himself off and then took a bead on Lawrence and Harvey, who were running this way and that in the near distance.

"Like shooting chickens in a henhouse . . ."

"Keep running, Lawrence!" Harvey shouted.

"Oh, Harvey, I don't want to die like a chicken!"

Hissing a laugh, Jim Crain steadied his sights on the skinny man, bringing him dead center.

To Harvey he shouted, "Don't worry, fat boy! Run as far as you want! I'll get to you soon enough!"

"Oh, Harvey!" Lawrence cried.

Crain tightened his finger on the trigger.

Over the hill rode John Slocum on his Appaloosa.

"What the—" Jim Crain hissed, swiveling instantly away from Lawrence to put Slocum in his sights.

But Slocum had already pulled off a shot, and then, aiming more carefully, pulled off another.

The Sharps rifle flew from Jim Crain's hands as he fell back dead, landing backside first in the hole he had just climbed out of.

"Hurray for Mr. Slocum!" Harvey said, stopping in his tracks.

"Is it over, Mr. Slocum?" Harvey asked.

Slocum, riding up beside Harvey Oliver, said, "Yep. It's over."

"Whew!" Harvey said.

"Mind if I ask you something?" Slocum said.

"Anything, Mr. Slocum!"

"If it's over, why is your dude friend there still running for his life?"

Harvey looked at his friend, still moving his legs madly, and called out, "Hey, Lawrence, you can come back now! Mr. Slocum's taken care of things!"

Lawrence continued to run, disappearing over the nearest hill.

"Lawrence! Come back!"

"No!" Lawrence called out.

"Why not!" Harvey shouted.

"Because I don't want to die like a chicken!"

Slocum said, "I'm sure that meant something."

Harvey, looking up at Slocum with a look of refined disgust, answered, "Don't count on it, Mr. Slocum."

38

Before too long, everyone except Lawrence Stanwell, who'd refused to stop running, had gathered in celebration inside the walls by the ruins of the ranch house of the Bar B Ranch.

Slocum and Harvey Olivier found a real party going on when they returned. Bentine met the two of them with glasses of whiskey, and pointed to the pile of ruins that had been at one time the ranch house.

"We've already talked about it, Soames and Corben and I, and we're going to build a new house right here for Mr. Lawrence and Mr. Stanwell. The whole town of Parsonage'll pass the hat for it, I'm sure. Miss Belinda knows a fancy lawyer and a judge from back in St. Louis, and she's going to get them to go over Forsen's papers. Before too long everyone that Forsen stole land from will have their ranches back."

He looked over the surrounding hills.

"Soon this town'll be just the way it started

out—a good place for people to live!"

He left them with their whiskey, and walked away to join the general party.

Slocum downed his whiskey, then took Harvey Olivier's when it was offered to him and downed that too.

"I don't drink whiskey, Mr. Slocum," Harvey explained. He twirled a finger over his head. "It makes my brain spin."

Looking past Harvey, Slocum said, "Looks like it makes your friend's brain spin too."

With alarm, Harvey looked around to see Lawrence Stanwell stumbling toward them. The rest of the group was already laughing at his antics. He held a bottle and was obviously drunk, and his head was covered in chicken feathers.

"What happened to you!" Harvey demanded.

Lawrence smiled inanely. "I figured if I was going to die like a chicken, I might as well die with them!"

He held the bottle up proudly.

"And what about that whiskey!" his fat friend asked.

Lawrence hiccuped, and nearly fell down, recovering at the last moment. "It was in the chicken coop! I guess the chickens wanted to die happy!"

He held the bottle up and smiled.

"Oh, what am I going to do with you!" Harvey said, exasperated, throwing his hands into the air.

Lawrence stumbled off, smiling, his fat friend following him to yell at him for his foolishness.

•   •   •

Slocum wandered over to where Helen Belinda stood alone, gazing over the wall toward her father's ranch.

She smiled up at Slocum and pointed.

"Looks like I'll be getting it back."

Slocum said, "I heard you'll be heading to St. Louis."

She nodded. "I'll take the girls back there to stay, and bring some real lawmen back with me. This town's going to straighten out and stay that way."

She looked into Slocum's eyes.

"Speaking of straight . . ."

Slocum smiled.

"Why, ma'am, I do believe you're having fun with me."

"I'd like to," Helen cooed.

"I do believe that could be arranged tonight, after this party winds down," Slocum said.

She kissed him lightly.

"Till tonight then," she said.

39

Night didn't come soon enough.

But finally the party was over, the revelers asleep either drunk or sober.

Slocum made his way out to his camp ground past Lawrence Stanwell, sleeping propped against the sleeping mule, Gladys, cradling his empty bottle, his head still covered in feathers, a wide smile on his face.

Helen Belinda was waiting for Slocum, the cloth of the bedroll pulled up to her chin.

"Modest, aren't we?" Slocum said.

She threw the bedroll aside, revealing the creamy nakedness she wore beneath.

"Not really." She laughed.

In a few moments Slocum had removed his clothing and lowered himself onto her.

"John, I *do* believe you're happy to be here," Helen said with a laugh.

"How can you tell?"

She reached down to take Slocum's hardening member in her gentle fingers.

"Let's just say I have physical evidence," she cooed.

Soon, under her expert guidance, Slocum was more than ready to oblige her request:

"Put it in deep, John," Helen moaned.

She opened, and slid Slocum's shaft into her waiting wetness, and once again they began to move against one another, Helen pulling him balls-deep into her hot recesses, smothering a moan of ecstasy each time Slocum's hard, huge love piston hit the very bottom of her love cave.

"Oh, John!"

She began to buck and sweat beneath him, grinding his swelling member, her own hot juice ready to burst forth.

"Together, John! Together!"

"Whatever you like, Helen," Slocum groaned.

He felt her coming, and let his own rising gorge break out of him at the exact moment she burst.

Like two cannons firing into each other, they roared, cum hitting cum in a flying hot mixture of sweet whiteness that went on and on. For each of Slocum's volleys she matched with one of her own—two, three, four—and at each burst of juice Helen literally thrust her middle off the ground as Slocum rammed himself down into her.

"John! Oh, John!"

Still she came, and still Slocum followed her in exact measure—five, six, seven—until they were nothing but a mass of white explosions in the night.

"John!" she screamed a final time, unable to cover her mouth against the fiery thrill she felt, as her last great volley blew into Slocum's own last explosion.

Helen collapsed on the ground, panting furiously, a glow suffusing her face under her sweat-matted hair.

"John . . ." she sighed.

Slocum smiled down at her.

Regaining her breath, she looked into Slocum's eyes deeply and said, "John, I've been thinking, you could come to St. Louis with me. I know you'll have to move on after that, but you could decide to ride that way, couldn't you?"

Slocum smiled and said, "I could certainly think about riding that way."

"Would you, John?" she said. "Would you at least think about it? We have to leave early tomorrow morning, but you could follow."

Slocum nodded. "I'll think about it."

"Good!"

And then another look came onto her face, and she smiled slightly and pressed her belly up against him. "And now . . ."

She once more snaked her hand down to find his love shaft.

Slocum already felt himself responding, and knew that it would be a long night.

40

It *was* a long night, and when Slocum awoke to blinding daylight the next day, Helen was gone.

Slocum packed up his Appaloosa, getting ready to ride out, and rode the short distance from his camp back into the ranch yard.

To Slocum's amazement, most of the wall had already been torn down, and a wagon load of new timber had already arrived and was being stacked near a cleared-out area next to the old ranch house.

"Mr. Slocum!" Harvey Oliver called, waving. "We're going to have a new house!"

Slocum dismounted and walked to where Harvey was wrestling with a length of wood, with the Mexican, Victor Herera, yelling at him in consternation.

"No, don't pick it up that way! What did I tell you!"

Harvey paused and said brightly, "Mr. Herera has decided to stay on with us and become partners!"

Herera looked at the sky, then at Slocum. He

smiled slightly. "If I don't go mad first, Mr. Slocum!"

"What time is it?" Slocum asked.

"Why, it's after noon!" Harvey said. "Mr. Corben went back to town and brought this lumber back a little while ago. Miss Belinda and the young ladies left just after dawn, and she said not to wake you, that you needed your sleep!"

Slocum said, "Where's Lawrence?"

With a sour look on his face, Harvey cocked his thumb at the tall pile of lumber.

"Hey, Lawrence!" Harvey called.

From behind the pile, Lawrence's haggard face rose.

Lawrence smiled wanly, waved, and began to rub at the top of his head with his fingers while he yawned.

"Get over here!" Harvey ordered.

Shrugging, Lawrence rose and stumbled toward them, falling over one of the timbers on the way.

Harvey Olivier turned to Slocum excitedly. "Oh, I almost forgot!"

He hurried away toward one of the wagons, and returned with a small box, which he handed to Slocum.

"Havanas?" Slocum said, taking the box.

Harvey nodded. "Mr. Corben brought them from the general store. He said Mr. Grierson would have wanted you to have them."

Slocum nodded in appreciation. "Thanks."

"You heading out now?"

Slocum nodded, and remounted his Appaloosa. "Yes, I think I am."

Harvey held out his hand for Slocum to shake. "We can't thank you enough, Mr. Slocum."

"There's no need." He turned to Victor Herera and smiled. "Make these boys work," he said.

Herera looked at the sky and mumbled.

Slocum laughed. "You know," he said, looking at Lawrence and Harvey, "I want to thank you dudes for something. Before I met you two, I think I was losing my sense of humor. Everything was looking mighty gray. But you two boys took care of that for me."

Harvey beamed, and Lawrence, hung over as he was, looked confused.

"Well, be seeing you," Slocum said, moving his Appaloosa off toward the Bar B Ranch sign, which had already been put back up.

"Good-bye, Mr. Slocum!" Harvey called.

"Yeah, good-bye and good luck!" Lawrence said.

Slocum waved.

"Hey, Mr. Slocum, where are you heading?" Harvey shouted.

Slocum thought for a second, and then said, "Think I'll head toward St. Louis."

He rode out in that direction, lighting up one of his new Havanas, hearing the somehow comforting sounds of banging and yelling behind him, of Harvey Olivier howling in pain and Lawrence Stanwell whining and crying, saying he was sorry.

Slocum smiled.

He knew that at this moment at least, because of laughter, the world was just a little better than it had been.

A special offer for people who enjoy reading the best Westerns published today.

WESTERNS!

NO OBLIGATION

Mail the coupon below

To start your subscription and receive 2 FREE WESTERNS, fill out the coupon below and mail it today. We'll send your first shipment which includes 2 FREE BOOKS as soon as we receive it.